GERALD PETIEVICH

MONEY MEN

PINNACLE BOOKS
WINDSOR PUBLISHING CORP.

This is a work of fiction. All the characters and events portrayed in this book are fictional, and any resemblance to real people or incidents is purely coincidental.

PINNACLE BOOKS

are published by

Windsor Publishing Corp.
475 Park Avenue South
New York, NY 10016

Third printing: August, 1988

Printed in the United States of America

☐ WASHINGTON, D.C. ☐

PETIEVICH'S TOUGH, LEAN PROSE RACES WITH THE ACTION. . . . but the dialogue snaps and crackles a la George Higgins and Eddie Coyle's friends! GRITTY! REALISTIC!

—Washington Post

☐ OREGON ☐

A TIGHT BUNDLE OF EXCITEMENT . . . PETIEVICH IS NOT JUST A SHOOT-EM-UP WRITER. HE HAS STYLE! And if it is presumptuous to be reminded of Hemingway, well, that happens to be the case. There are myriad novels being published, but someone made a fine discovery with Petievich, and we feel Carr will be with us for some time, creating legends and giving us a peek at human realities behind the vaulted doors of the Treasury Department.

—The Oregonian

☐ HOUSTON ☐

SUSPENSEFUL YET FUN AND EASY TO READ. . . . The strength is realism—in characters, in the streets on which they operate, and in these devious operations themselves. GERALD PETIEVICH KNOWS WHEREOF HE WRITES!

—The Houston Post

☐ OHIO ☐

ACTION-PACKED . . . AUTHENTICITY!

—The Cleveland Press

☐ MASSACHUSETTS ☐

THE AUTHENTIC RING OF AN AUTHOR WHO HAS SEEN CRIME FIRST-HAND! Hard-boiled American-style sex and violence.
—*The Patriot Ledger*
(Quincy, Mass.)

☐ MISSISSIPPI ☐

CRISP AND HARD-HITTING! GIVE GERALD PETIEVICH A DARN GOOD SHOT AT BECOMING A CHANDLER! . . . I never thought I would see the day I might, just might, compare a new writer of detective fiction with somebody I felt was the best ever . . . but (Petievich) writes in the same spare prose Chandler used in his Philip Marlowe stories. The endings are logically clever . . . carefully worked out and, at the same time, spontaneous. We may well find, one day soon, the names Charlie Carr and Gerald Petievich ranking high in library shelves under "fiction—detective," and we will be the better for it, if so. Relaxation with a good detective novel now and then is good for the soul.
—*The Natchez Democrat*

☐ AND MORE ☐

A DIVERTING SCAM . . . Old fashioned crime yarns (with) good, gritty dialogue!
—*Kirkus Reviews*

STRAIGHTFORWARD, INTERESTING, RE-ALISTIC, HARD-HITTING, AND SUSPENSE-FUL! If this isn't the way Treasury Agents live and work and counterfeiting operations take place, Mr. Petievich has done a remarkable job of convincing us otherwise!
—*Best Sellers*

To Pam

MONEY
MEN

The tiny motel room had the odor of mildewed carpet. Charles Carr waited, peeking out occasionally through the yellowed Venetian blind at the room Rico was in. An ancient air conditioner rattled outside the window, filtering warm August smog into cool August smog.

Carr's partner, Jack Kelly, slouched on the bed in rumpled suit and tie, watching the Johnny Carson show on a television set that was bolted and chained to the wall. The room needed painting, and the ceiling mirror reflected a stained bedspread with a cigarette burn.

Each time Carr peeked out he could see the neon sign. It proclaimed SUNSET MOTEL—WATERBEDS, TV, FREE ICE, as if the hookers and their johns who slithered in and out of the rooms cared about such extras. Carr preferred to use the Sunset for undercover operations because the rooms were easy to observe from either of the buildings that faced each other across a small parking lot.

Across Sunset Boulevard was a dingy hot-dog stand surrounded by Hollywood's new breed: runaways with no bras, shirtless punks in vests, skinny men dressed as women. Farther down the street a dwarf hawked phony maps to movie stars' homes.

He remembered bringing dates twenty years—even ten years—ago to the classy theaters on Hollywood Boulevard, stopping for a drink near Grauman's Chinese.

Now, he saw the town as a population of crooks and victims. The street people had taken over. The old ladies who lived on the side streets had either moved to Newport Beach or put up wrought-iron window bars.

In fact, eight years ago, when he had first met Sally, she had lived in an apartment in Hollywood. A while back, when she had moved to an apartment near his in Santa Monica, she said it was because of the steet people. But Carr knew that was only part of it. She had wanted him to get used to her being close. It had worked.

He wanted to call her tonight, but didn't know quite what to say. He didn't look forward to the explanation of why he hadn't phoned in almost a month. There was no particular reason except that he had been busy making arrests because of Rico. Plenty of arrests: pimps and pushers, blacks and whites, anyone who had counterfeit money for sale.

The underworld had bought Rico hook, line, and sinker. It had been Carr's idea to give Rico plenty of leeway, and it had worked. Rico's answering-service phone hadn't stopped ringing for a month. The word of a solid buyer had spread fast. The project chart showed twenty-one separate hand-to-hand buys in a month. Twenty-one trips to the federal lockup for the sellers. Even in court, with Rico on the witness stand, some of them had difficulty believing the surly Rico was a United States Treasury special agent.

"Why cause misery?" Kelly said during a commercial. "Ever think of it like that?" He folded meat-hook hands behind his head. "Everything we do causes shit for somebody. You get a call to a liquor store . . . somebody passed a phony twenty. You give the liquor-store man a receipt for the twenty. He is pissed off. You find the guy who passed the twenty and arrest him. He is pissed off. You find the printer and arrest him. Now you have enemies. In court the federal prosecutor doesn't like the case, so he's pissed off, and the judge hates you on general principles. So I ask you: Why should we break our ass making cases? Why cause misery?"

"Because it's a lot of good clean fun," Carr said, with a wry smile.

"Yeah, and so is cancer," said Kelly.

Carr looked at his watch. It was 11:30 P.M. He tested the volume knob on the Kel Kit radio receiver on the table next to him. If the batteries held out, he would be able to hear every word in Rico's room.

Straddling a chair, he leaned closer to the Venetian blind. He removed the gold Treasury badge from his pocket and clipped it to his coat pocket so it would be in plain sight for the arrest.

The radio receiver blared. Rico's voice was young and upper Bronx. "I'll make the phone call now," Rico said. "Better tell Kelly to wake up." He laughed.

"Wise ass," Kelly said to the television.

Rico dialed the phone.

"Hello, Ronnie? This is Angelo," said the young

3

undercover agent. "I got your message. I'll see you in room seven at the Sunset Motel near California Street within a half hour. I'm ready to deal and I'm not going to wait any longer than thirty minutes . . . Right . . . I will show you my ten-grand buy money before you show me the funny money . . . You have nothing to worry about if what you deliver is like the sample you gave me."

Good job, Carr thought. Set the time limit and the rules.

The waterbed made a sloshing sound as Kelly lumbered off it. He looked a little like an old bear. The parts of his body were oversized. Enormous hands and feet, big nose and jowls.

"Sounds like your star pupil is catching on," he said, tucking in his shirt.

Carr nodded and stuck his hand in front of the Venetian blind, giving Rico the thumbs-up sign. Rico returned the gesture, then closed the curtain of his room; standard procedure.

The bedsprings creaked. Rico sat down on the bed in his room to wait. Everything having been planned, everyone having been briefed, there was nothing else to say. The arrest signal would be the usual one. Rico would say, "That seems to be all of it," after he had counted the counterfeit money. Then the door would go down.

"Does Rico have an undercover piece?" Kelly said.

"Two inch in an ankle holster," Carr said. The question caused him to reflect for a moment on the fact that he had found it necessary to remind Rico of safety precautions a little too often. He had chalked this up to the "Elliot Ness syndrome," which he had surmounted over twenty years ago.

He figured everyone went through it. Running a finger through flame.

"You know why Rico's been doing so well in this project?" Kelly fiddled with the handcuffs on his belt.

"Why?"

"Because he looks more like a crook than the people who sell him the counterfeit money. Olive complexion, black hair, pinky ring; a real Richard Conte."

"He's too young to know who Richard Conte is," said Carr as he stared out the window at the hot-dog-stand freaks.

"Walking entrapment. That's what Rico is. Some shyster will probably bring that up as a defense someday." Kelly lowered his voice. "Ladies and gentlemen of the jury, look at this mean-looking Italian. He scared my poor client into selling him counterfeit money. How's that for a defense?" Kelly rubbed his barrel stomach. "I'm hungry," he said.

"He sounded real nervous over the phone," Rico said. The transmitter gave his voice a hollow, metallic tone.

Carr wished he could say something back, thought for a moment of phoning Rico's room, but decided against it. The seller would be arriving any minute.

Kelly peeked out the opposite end of the Venetian blind. "This room smells like the dog pound. They should rename this place the Dog Shit Motel. The Hollywood Dog Shit Motel."

Carr shook his head.

Over the radio came the sound of Rico lighting a cigarette.

5

Kelly began pacing around the room to kill time, running his hand through his salt-and-pepper hair at regular intervals.

"There he is!" said Carr. A young man carrying an attaché case approached Rico's room. The man appeared to be about thirty, medium build, and wore a stylish black leather jacket. He glanced behind him nervously.

Standing at the door, Kelly undid the inside latch and tested the handle, making sure it was unlocked. He pulled his revolver from the shoulder holster and held it next to his leg.

The man in the leather jacket took a final look behind him and knocked on the door. He went in.

Carr turned up the radio.

"Well, here I am," said the man. There was a quaver in his voice. "I've got the funny money right here in the case. Let's see the real stuff."

"Take it easy," Rico said. "I've got the ten grand . . . Look."

Carr heard the crinkling of the paper bag he had given Rico earlier containing Uncle Sam's marked ten thousand dollars. He guessed Rico had poured the money out on the bed for the count.

Carr turned the volume on the radio even higher. There was the unsnapping of the latches on the attaché case . . . a frenzied moment of scrambling. A loud blast made him jump out of his chair. He instinctively pulled his gun. Ears throbbing, he dashed out the door and across the parking lot to Rico's room, Kelly a few feet behind.

Attacking the motel door with powerful kicks, they entered the room guns first.

Rico was lying on the floor next to the bed,

hands clutching his face. Kelly ran to the open window.

No one else was in the room.

Tires squealed outside. "He's gone!" screamed Kelly. He ran to the phone.

Revolver still in hand, Carr moved closer to Rico and began to kneel down. He was involuntarily repulsed. Rico's face was blown back and away like a skinned rabbit. A distorted eye socket was gouged open to meet the ear, and bits of brain matter and blood made a circular design on the corner of the cheap bedspread.

Carr, on his knees, stared at the ruined body.

Kelly yelled, gasped, into the phone, "I want an ambulance! Sunset Motel, Sunset at California Street! A federal officer has been shot."

Carr placed his fingers gently on Rico's neck. No pulse. No breathing. He stared at his fingers, now wet with blood.

Rico's pants leg was up and the small revolver, the undercover gun, was showing. It was still in the holster.

Kelly stood next to him and crossed himself. "Holy Mother of God," he cried, turning his head away. "He must have used a sawed-off shotgun."

To Carr, the squalid room become more unbearable with each group that arrived: ambulance attendants shaking their heads, young policemen running about, and, finally, coroner's deputies in olive-drab overalls.

Later, as police detectives and Treasury agents cordoned off the motel room, combing for evidence, Carr and Kelly stood together outside the door. They were unable to look at one another.

The motel lot was full of men and women who had come out of their rooms to gape.

Across the boulevard the habitués of the hot-dog stand pointed and gawked like children watching a puppet show.

A coroner's ghoul walked from a black station wagon carrying a blue rubber body bag.

"Don't use that," Carr said.

"Whaddaya mean?" mumbled the ghoul. He looked at Carr's eyes for a moment.

"Oh, yeah, sure."

A few minutes later Carr stepped out of the way as the man pushed the gurney toward the station wagon. The body of Rico de Fiore was wrapped in a sheet and blanket.

The fatigue had set in.

On the way back to Hollywood from downtown, Carr leaned back in the passenger seat and closed his eyes. Kelly weaved in and out of freeway traffic and rambled fitfully about the lack of clues.

Though early in the morning, it was already hot enough to turn on air conditioning or jump in a pool. They had been up all night, going from county morgue to field office to police department; a headachy night of repeating the story, making reports, phone calls, composite sketches. Kelly pulled into a no-parking curb zone in front of Rico's apartment building. A sign posted in the middle of an ivy lawn read APARTMENT FOR RENT. ADULTS ONLY—NO PETS.

Carr opened a window inside the studio apartment, thus furnishing the room with a shaft of dust-reflecting light and a view of a cement re-

8

taining wall. "When you rent a place, make sure there are no windows facing the street," Carr had told Rico, as if the young agent hadn't known better.

The furniture was neat and impersonal: a painted chest of drawers, flower-patterned sofa, and small wooden desk. On the wall above the sofa hung a desert-scene print in an aluminum frame, which came with the room.

The apartment reminded Carr of scores of the easily forgetable "temporary duty" places he had rented in his early career. A trailer in Las Vegas, the two-bedroom hovel in San Francisco's mission district, a brownstone walk-up in Baltimore; the duty was temporary because it ended when everyone except the undercover man was suddenly arrested. He remembered the loneliness brought on as much by the environment of self-interest as by solitude. He had learned to take the edge off the loneliness by working harder, meeting more paper pushers, pressing more strongly for the hundred-grand buys.

Kelly rummaged through pots and pans in the kitchen. He pulled a large roaster pan from a bottom drawer of the stove and removed the lid. "Here's the issue equipment," he said. He sat down at a chrome-legged dinette table and removed items from the roaster pan: a government-issued cassette tape recorder with telephone attachment, a shoulder holster, binoculars, expense voucher forms, government transportation requests. He put the items in a cardboard box.

Carr found one of Rico's phony driver's licenses hidden under army-rolled socks in the chest of drawers. He picked it up and handed it to Kelly.

9

Carr remembered picking Rico up at the airport two months ago and handing him the license. "Don't forget to memorize the date of birth on the license before you fill out the rental application," he had said. It was always the little things.

Kelly was up and crashing about, pulling drawers out of cupboards, turning them upside down, spilling things. "His daily reports have got to be here somewhere."

"They're here somewhere," Carr said.

He had met Rico late every night at the hot-dog stand on Alvarado to check them. Rico's reports were always up to date.

Carr had said, "Keep the pressure on. Make the seller put up or shut up. It's what real crooks do. Make 'em deliver and give the arrest signal. You know the scenario and they don't. Keep it simple."

"You like to play with their minds," Rico said. "All I want to do is make a few buys, testify before the grand jury, and go home to New York. Times Square at midnight is kindergarten compared to temporary duty in Hollywood." They both laughed.

Rico was the best he had seen—cautious, with the ability to take orders, but, more important, the ability to break them if necessary, to be resourceful, to recognize things as they were and forget the always safe and sure *Manual of Operations* answer. Like Carr, Rico could feel the pulse.

Kelly, trancelike, sat down at the kitchen table again. He talked into the cardboard box.

Then he slammed a fist into an open palm. "Sheeyit!"

$12

Carr, a trim man with mournful brown eyes, wove his way through flocks of Chinatown tourists. The smell of incense and fried shrimp was familiar. He headed for Ling's Bar, passing novelty shops with bored-looking Oriental sales people standing in doorways. Having just come from the funeral, he needed a drink.

He paused and noticed his reflection in the window glass of a jade-jewelry shop. He was shocked by his seedy, tired appearance. Darkness under the eyes and a sprinkle of broken blood vessels on his cheekbones. Features fighting age. Temples more gray than brown. Maybe a haircut would help, and perhaps a shoeshine.

Or maybe a new wardrobe. . . . His lapels were outdated. He refused to buy new suits to look stylish while crawling under a house to search for counterfeit money or wrestling a hype.

His appearance had been one of Sally's pet topics. She had even given him a hair blower. He had used it once and retired it to a junk drawer.

As he waited for the light at Hill Street, he thought of the bright stained glass, agents and cops standing in line, the sound of Rico's sisters sobbing.

The light turned green and he continued on, crossing the street among a group of middle-aged women. Hell, he was close to their age. Behind him were twenty years of "street time."

Staying on the street, with his sleeves rolled up, had been his own choice. Asking questions and getting answers was what he was good at, climbing the ladder to the printing press, beating the bad guys. Leave the pencil-pushing to those who took their transfers to the ivory tower of Washington, D.C.

Now, things had changed. Because of Rico's murder he knew he was headed for the barn. The first rule of bureaucracy is that somebody always has to take the blame. They would say that his security precautions at the motel had not been adequate. They would transfer him to the Washington, D.C., scrap heap. Had he done the right thing by refusing the promotions that had been offered him through the years?

He passed a penny-stained goldfish pond known as the Chinatown Wishing Well and turned down an alley.

"Charlie!"

A man's voice behind him. Higgins, a muscular man with short blond hair, walked toward him down the alley with a paper napkin tucked over his belt buckle. His pants were baggy and he wore a plaid sports coat with a revolver bulge on the right side. Approaching Carr, he pulled the napkin from his belt and wiped his mouth.

"Just chowing down," he said. "Saw you pass by the window. I need to run one by ya."

"Shoot," Carr said.

"I'm looking for a guy who slit an old lady's throat. Snitch says the guy who did it has a nickname—'Trash-Truck Jimmy.' S'posed to have done time years ago for passing queer twenties and tens. Ring a bell?"

"Jimmy Tortamasi," Carr said. "He did time in Terminal Island about five years ago for passing. Escaped once by hiding inside a trash truck. He walks with a limp now. The truck had a hydraulic compacter, and he figured there was enough room for a body between the pusher and the back wall of the truck."

"I take it he figured wrong."

"Right," Carr said. "It crushed him like a grape. After a year in the prison hospital he was good as new . . . except for the leg. Jimmy should be about forty-five now. When he's out of the joint, he usually lives in one of the fleabags around McArthur Park."

Higgins was writing the name down on the napkin. "T-o-r-t-a-m-a-s-i-?" he said.

Carr nodded.

"I told my partner, if the dude was into bad paper, you'd know who he was." He put the napkin in his shirt pocket and stepped a little closer to Carr. Suddenly he looked embarrassed. "I'm sorry about Rico. I didn't get a chance to make it to the funeral. . . ."

"I want to know everything you hear about capers with sawed-off shotguns. Call me night or day."

"That's a promise," said the detective.

Carr swung open the door at Ling's, and glass chimes rattled. Sunlight splashed along the bar,

revealing rows of brandy snifters with tiny para-
sols. On the wall hung a swan-scene tapestry and a
photograph of the spectacled Ling and his brother
wearing bow ties.

A dusty jukebox in the corner (known to the
badge-carrying regular as Ling's Hit Parade)
waited to blend outdated tunes into the usual
field office and precinct house chatter. Because of
the early hour, the four worn Naugahyde booths
nestled against the opposite wall were empty.

Delgado sat at the bar alone. He stood up and
greeted Carr with a strong handshake. He had
been the agent-in-charge in Los Angeles years
ago, before his leadership abilities had vaulted
him to Washington, D.C.

It was no secret that Delgado and Carr were old
friends. Without a friend in Washington, Carr
could never have managed to avoid the bureau-
crat's obsessive love of transfers and remain in Los
Angeles. Of course, wanting to stay in Los Angeles
was a desire few other agents could understand.
While most other T-men couldn't wait to buy a set
of golf clubs and ship out for three years of "eight-
a-day-Monday-through-Friday" in Phoenix or
Portland, Carr preferred L.A.'s big-city action.
Undercover buys, search warrants, and conspiracy
cases were his cup of tea. Besides, Los Angeles,
from sandy-floored beach bars to the shady edges
of the tract-house valleys, felt like home by now.

"Greetings, *amigo*," said the tall, slim Chicano.
"It's been a long time." With his full head of gray
hair and pin-striped suit, Alex Delgado could pass
for a Latin-American diplomat.

"I guess you knew where to find me," Carr said.

14

"Right." Delgado laughed curtly. "I came here from the airport. . . . Took the noon flight out of Dulles." He looked ill-at-ease. His complexion had a saddle-soap tinge.

Carr sat down. He looked at the other man's suit. "You dress a little better now that you're a big-shot headquarters inspector," he said with a smile.

"I'm such a big shot that I'm bored to death. My job is nothing but political bullshit, staff reports, and phony statistics . . . Doctor tells me I have an ulcer." Delgado pointed to his glass. "Look at me. I have to drink Scotch and milk. I had an operation, but it didn't help, so I've been thinking about pulling the pin. I've got my twenty-five years in, and I'm tired of fighting the ass kissers and pencil heads. . . ." He tore pieces from the wet napkin under his drink. "How about you?"

Ling set a Scotch-and-water in front of Carr, who sipped, then said, "Haven't really thought about it."

"Are you still seeing Sally?"

Carr nodded.

"Nice gal. A really classy lady. The wife and I always sort of hoped you two would get married. You go back a long ways with Sally, don't you?"

"I guess so."

"Typical Charlie Carr remark," Delgado said. "Noncommital when it comes to anything personal. No, sir, you haven't changed a bit."

"You have. You used to get to the point a little quicker."

Delgado ignored the statement without so much as a wince. A survival technique, Carr figured, that

15

he had picked up at the School of Beating Around the Bush on the banks of the Potomac; smile, agree, ignore, achieve.

The gray-haired man dug a handkerchief out of his pocket and wiped milk from the corners of his mouth. "I look at retirement as just a change of scenery," he said. "Nothing more. It'll do me good. I don't need the pressure any more. I've done my part. It'll be a welcome change for me. Changes are something we all have to face." He gulped the chalky mixture and continued. "It's just a matter of accepting the stages of life. I mean you and I are of another generation. The new guys don't know how it was years ago, before court decisions: Miranda, Escobedo, outlawing the wiretaps. . . . Things are one hundred percent different from when you and I went to Special Agent School. I'm sure you agree."

Carr didn't answer.

"Seriously. I'm asking your opinion," Delgado said. He patted Carr's arm.

Carr looked at Ling and made the "another round" gesture with his index finger. Ling dug into a sink full of ice with a scoop.

"Nothing has changed," Carr said. "It's the same street, the same bad guys. The same rules. Only difference is that they don't stay in prison as long—and they all carry guns. That's because they watch TV and they think they are *supposed* to carry guns. Other than that, nothing has changed. Everything is exactly the same."

Delgado curtly laughed away from the subject and steered the conversation to small talk. The next two hours were spent talking of ancient cases, almost forgotten girlfriends, and snapping fingers

16

trying to remember bartenders' names at some of the old downtown hangouts.

Though it was one drink after another, neither man became drunk. It was as if it was necessary to pour in the drinks to continue. Carr knew it was Delgado's way.

Then finally came the trunk story. It was almost a ritual between them by now and seemed to grow with every retelling. Undereover Agent Carr, acting the part of a buyer and convincing the seller to accompany him to Big Bear to pick up a package of twenties, Delgado hiding in the trunk of the automobile as protection. Delgado's motion sickness on the mountain roads, the retching sounds coming from the trunk, Carr turning up the radio to cover the sounds—then the punch line. Delgado, covered from head to toe with vomit, jumps out of the trunk, gun drawn, and runs into the mountain cabin to arrest the counterfeiter. When it was over, even *he* had laughed at Delgado's strange appearance.

They chuckled. Delgado slapped Carr on the back. "Charlie, you're one of the best undercover men in Treasury. For twenty years you've made cases that others couldn't make. The counterfeiters fear you. You're known as the Snake out there. . . . He sipped a fresh Scotch-and-milk. "But guys like you and me have to move along in life. . . . Do you know what I'm saying?"

"Not exactly," Carr said. I'm going to make you say it, he thought.

"I'm telling you the powers-that-be are saying that Charlie the Snake should accept his rightful senior agent status like the others of his vintage and come out of the street. I mean why the hell should you still be out there booting doors, covering buys, taking chances every goddamn day? In that, I agree with what they are saying."

Ling served Carr's seventh Scotch-and-water with a "here comes joke" leer, and said something about Carr's needing to find a new girlfriend since Rose the cocktail waitress was on vacation at Lake Arrowhead. Carr forced a smile. Ling returned to a sink at the other end of the bar and continued scrubbing glasses.

"I guess you know that I'm in charge of the shooting investigation," Delgado said. "That's why they sent me out here."

Carr took a long pull from the drink. "What have they decided to do with me?"

Delgado paused before answering. "Charlie, you know I'm just the one who coordinates the interviews and writes the final report. I can make a recommendation, but what happens in the end is up to the people at headquarters."

"Hogwash," Carr said matter-of-factly. "The Ivory Tower has already decided what they're going to do. Your report will be justification for it. I want to know what's going to happen to me."

Delgado looked at his drink sadly. "They're going to transfer you on the next list. Of course you'll be able to get your choice of offices. . . . I can help with that."

Carr spoke to Delgado's reflection in the bar mirror. "Hold up the transfer until I find who killed Rico."

"You know how headquarters is. . . ."

Carr turned to face the other man. "To hell with headquarters. I'm not taking a transfer until this thing is over."

"No, sir, the years haven't changed Charlie Carr." Delgado sipped his drink. He rubbed his stomach.

Carr felt uneasy. He wished he'd been less direct.

"Charlie, what are your ideas on how the investigation should go?" Delgado said at last.

"If Rico's murder had made the papers," Carr said, "we might never find the killer. Luckily, there's been no publicity, so the killer must believe he murdered a hood. He must figure that the cops have nothing to go on except the body of a thief in a motel room. I say that's what we want him to think. Let him believe he killed a hood rather than a cop. Our only chance to bag him is if he tries it again."

Delgado nodded and ordered more drinks.

At 1:30 A.M. Ling began wiping up the bar and locking liquor cabinets. He yammered something about closing time.

"I guess you were pretty close to the young fellow," said Delgado in a soft tone.

Carr cleared his throat twice. "You would have liked him. He was one-hundred-percent T-man. He could have become an inspector like you someday. He could smell green ink a mile away." He spoke imploringly, as if the inspector had the power to change what had happened.

"I'm going to lay my cards on the table," Delgado said, with open palms. "I want the killer caught one way or the other. You know what I mean by that. On the other hand, I don't want to see you end up in Leavenworth in his place."

Delgado got off his barstool, rushed his drink to his mouth, and swallowed. He looked at Carr. "I

19

can postpone your transfer for a few weeks. It's against policy, but I've got my years in and there's not a hell of a lot they can do to me at this point. I'll use the argument that you are the only one who saw the killer and can identify him. All I'm asking you to do is keep your head. I want your word you will keep your head."

Carr, sober, looked him in the eye. "You have my word."

"Ling, two more for the road," Delgado said.

"I'll also give you my word on something else," said Carr. "I'm going to find the one who did it and put him in a box."

Delgado acted as if he hadn't heard the remark.

Carr pushed the buzzer under the name Sally Malone and waited. He was prepared for her not to let him in.

Seconds later, the door buzzed open. He walked upstairs to her apartment. The door was ajar and he walked in almost cautiously. The living room was neat-as-a-pin Mediterranean, with lots of carved wood and modern-art prints. The place was as immaculate as her desk in Judge Malcolm's courtroom.

Sally was standing at the stove stirring mushrooms with a wooden spoon, her back to him. She wore a robe that barely touched her knees.

"Look who's here," she said without turning around. Her voice was soft, almost inaudible, as always.

Carr sat down at the kitchen table and drummed his fingers. Sally stopped stirring, poured a Scotch-and-water and plunked it down in front of him.

20

"You know this is the first time I have seen you in three weeks," she said after returning to the stove. Admiring her gray-streaked hair and tanned athletic features, Carr thought she looked much more like a dance instructor than a stenographer. They had met because she had asked *him* to lunch, during a counterfeiting trial. He remembered waiting for her to call him the next week, as sort of a people experiment. He finally had to call her. Later, she said she would never have called him for the second date. He always wondered. . . .

"You know how busy . . ." he said

She turned to faced him. "How busy can someone be!" she interrupted in an angry whisper. "Can you really be so busy that we only see each other once a month? . . . Twelve times a year? The same thing is happening to us again, and I, for one, should know better. Sometimes I can't believe I have known you for eight years."

"It's not like I intentionally didn't call you," Carr said. "You know that." He realized it was a dumb thing to say as soon as the words left his mouth.

"I know *exactly* why you didn't call! You and that crude Jack Kelly are like children who forget what time it is when they're playing. You get a charge out of arresting people and all the crap that goes with it. You are a forty-five-year-old Boy Scout! You like the danger or something. I don't understand you . . . Did you know that we both live in apartments in Santa Monica and see each other once a month? Oh, hell, what's the use!"

She turned back toward the stove, picked up the frying pan, and dumped the mushrooms into the sink. She washed the pan furiously. Nothing was said for a few minutes.

"Did you know the young undercover man who was killed? I heard the judge talking about it." Her tone was sour.

"Yes," murmured Carr. He sipped his drink.

Sally finished up at the stove and placed the utensils in the sink. She grabbed the edge of the kitchen counter with her hands and stood with her head down.

Carr looked at his watch. "I thought we could go to a movie tonight," he said politely.

"Jesus," she said, shaking her head. "No communication *whatsoever*. Why can't you talk to me? I heard you were *there* when it happened. Can't you at least share that with me? Sometimes when I am around you I feel absolutely alone, as if I'm talking to . . ."

Carr stood up and walked toward the door.

"Please don't leave right now," Sally said.

Quietly, Carr followed her into the bedroom.

It was the usual sex scene: the almost perfunctory kisses, clothes in neat separate piles, thrusting tongues, moans of love, her fingernails in the usual place on his shoulders, Carr delaying his orgasm until the proper time . . . Then the whispers.

"I have two tickets to a charity brunch a Marina Del Rey tomorrow morning," she said. "The judge gave them to me. It should be a real nice affair." She got up from the bed and put on a robe. Her eyes sought his reaction.

"I had planned to drive out . . ."

" . . . to Chino," she interrupted. "A two-hour drive to Chino prison to see Howard. After all, you certainly wouldn't want to miss your Saturday visit with him. You've gone out there every Saturday for the past year. Every single Saturday . . . Incredible." She shook her head.

"We could go somewhere on Sunday," Carr said.

She stared at the bedroom mirror. "Sure. To wherever I want. You, as usual, never have any ideas. For once I would like to go somewhere that we both want to go. . . . Though I'm sure you'd much prefer to be sitting in a bar in Chinatown drinking with your pals." She said "pals" as if it were a curse.

$3

Carr's mind wandered as he drove on the Pomona Freeway toward Chino. He pictured Norbert Waeves (known as No Waves), the pipe-smoking Los Angeles special agent-in-charge, puffing smoke and reading aloud the one-inch newspaper article about Howard. "Howard Dumbrowski, a special agent of the U.S. Treasury Department, pleaded guilty to manslaughter today in Superior Court. Accused of murdering his wife after finding her with another man in their Glendale apartment, Dumbrowski declined to make any statement in his own behalf before being sentenced to two years in state prison." Jumping for joy, the SAIC had tossed the newspaper in the air. "Hooray! He pleaded guilty! No trial! No more bad publicity!"

The visiting-hour trips to Chino were rough at the beginning—forced laughs followed by embarrassing silences.

Carr turned off the highway at the green overhead sign CALIFORNIA CORRECTIONAL INSTITUTE, CHINO. ONE MILE.

The visitors' area was in the open. Metal picnic

tables surrounded by a high chain-link fence. It reminded Carr of a grammar-school lunch area. At the tables sat blacks and Chicanos talking with sadly dressed wives. Restless children in T-shirts and tennis shoes wrestled on the yellow grass like bear cubs.

Howard, with a gray crew cut and starched denims, still looked like a cop: stocky, blue-bearded, piercing blue eyes. During the past year his eyes had seemed to become more deep-set.

Carr sat down. Howard smiled. He began dealing gin rummy, a ritual that started as a compromise to avoid the hurt of conversation. Howard had nothing to talk about any more, and Carr knew that shop talk, even about the old days, brought a sadness to Howard's eyes.

"I got a letter from my daughter yesterday. She told me about Rico de Fiore."

Carr hesitated. "I was his cover. The guy who did it got away from me. He jumped out the motel-room back window."

"Rico was a sharp kid. He had the touch," said the prisoner.

Carr nodded. They looked at each other for a moment.

Howard shuffled and dealt the cards. "Pick up your hand," he said.

At the end of the hand Carr took a small notebook out of his sports-coat pocket, turned to a fresh page, and recorded the score of the fiftieth game.

"I'm going to Eugene, Oregon, when I get out," Howard said. "Lumber-mill job. With the conviction, I figure that's the best I can do. I know I would have beat the rap if I'd gone to trial. Catch-

ing her in the sack and all, you know . . .
temporary insanity . . . But I didn't want to embarrass my daughter with a trial. You can imagine
how the press would have played up the whole
thing, how it would have looked to her college
friends."

Nothing was said for a long while. Eventually
Carr took over as dealer, Howard as scorekeeper.

"Partner, there's something I gotta say," Howard said. The blue eyes flashed. "There were
rough times in here, particularly the first few
months. I had to fight every day. Once, I found
out they were going to put ant poison in my chow.
I didn't eat until I found out who it was. A big
husky guy. I caught him in the yard and kicked
his teeth out. Got almost all of 'em." He hesitated.
"I guess what I'm getting at is that I don't know if
I would have made it without the card games. I
know I can make it now."

"Pick up your cards," Carr said.

"There's something else," Howard said. "Since
the day I was arrested, you're the only one who's
stuck by me, and you've never asked me one question about it. I really appreciate that. . . . But I
want you to know. A year ago I walked into my
apartment with a few drinks under my belt and
my old lady is fucking the next-door neighbor. I
killed her because I had my gun on. I was a federal
cop and my gun was right there in a holster on my
belt. Now I'm in the joint for it . . . but I'm the
same now as I ever was, and like you and everybody else in the whole goddamn world, I'm never
going to change. . . . My wife is dead and I'm
alive and one year older. It's as simple as that. A
set of circumstances."

27

A bell sounded. A guard opened a gate in the chain-link fence, and visitors began to depart.

Howard stood up and put the deck of cards in his shirt pocket. They shook hands. "Drop me a line when you get your transfer orders," Howard said.

The Treasury field office was located in the stodgy-looking Federal Courthouse on Spring street, just a few blocks up from L.A.'s skid row. Jack Kelly waited in the technical shop. He gazed out the window.

The view from the field office was clear, up to a point. Things over a half-mile or so away were blurry. Boyle Heights was in haze the color of oatmeal.

Below, on Spring Street, the "Blue Goose," a large police van, headed toward the tenderloin. Years ago, when Kelly had been on the force, the old-timers used to make the recruits drive the Goose, to avoid the body lice.

He looked at his watch and sipped coffee. For some reason he thought of the Timmy Fontaine incident.

He remembered being on the duty desk the night a young ponytailed hitchhiker marched into the field office and told him about how she was picked up by a "Timmy," who drove her to his Malibu bachelor pad, which had two giant stereo speakers.

After she posed for photos in the bedroom, Timmy masturbated while standing over her (Kelly remembered her describing this as being "far out") and then showed her a suitcase full of phony ten-dollar bills. Probably to show off.

Later, the brass said that before Kelly went to a federal judge and obtained a search warrant, he should have determined who Timmy was. The second-guessers figured that if Kelly had known that young Timmy was the son of the Honorable Augustus Fontaine (D., Calif.) he might have handled it differently.

That's where they were wrong. Jack Kelly wouldn't have cared if it had been Prince Charles with the suitcase full of green. He would have done exactly the same thing. Filed the search warrant, knocked on Timmy's door, announced his purpose, kicked Timmy's door down, found the suitcase, and arrested Timmy for possession of funny money, just as though he were any other street punk.

Just that alone would have started a major flap, but it burst into epic proportions when Timmy made the mistake of punching Kelly on the side of the head, during the arrest, breaking a manicured thumb. Kelly counterpunched the unfortunate Timmy on the point of the chin, breaking the attached jaw in two places and causing Timmy's mouth to be wired shut during the trial.

The pressure from above hadn't worked on the judge, and Timmy was sentenced to a year in Lompoc, which Kelly attributed to the fact that the judge had been appointed by a Republican administration.

The honorable congressman got back at them by having one of his old law partners sue Kelly and Uncle Sam in a trumped-up civil-rights and personal-injury case. They even alleged that Kelly broke Timmy's thumb in order to make him talk.

The suit failed, but Kelly ended up in cold storage indexing counterfeit notes and answering calls from bank tellers about what to do if "In God We Trust" was missing from the reverse of a twenty-dollar bill.

After a year he was offered a chance to return to field duties, but he told the agent-in-charge thanks anyway, but that he got the same pay for pushing a pencil as for cracking heads, and that he preferred to remain behind the desk.

It was Carr who had kept Kelly's interest piqued. He eventually enticed Kelly away from the desk and back into the street by little things, such as making sure that copies of interesting reports crossed his desk. Kelly knew what he was up to. Carr was his only real friend.

When Carr walked in now, he removed a cassette tape and a plastic envelope containing a counterfeit ten-dollar bill from a file folder marked "Evidence."

Kelly pushed aside a radio chassis and other odds and ends on the workbench and plugged in the tape recorder. He had heard the motel recording many times during the past three days, but realized that when other leads don't pan out a man has to start all over again.

The hours he and Carr had spent looking through mug books of known strong-arm men and rip-off artists had been useless.

They had read the reports of interviews with the residents of the street facing the rear of the motel. No one had seen anything out of the ordinary.

At the Police Crime Lab Kelly had been told there was no physical evidence. No footprints, no fingerprints, no hair. The man in the black leather jacket had walked in the door of the motel room, killed Rico, stolen the buy money, and departed like an actor in the final scene of some bizarre stage play.

Sure, Kelly knew he and Carr had seen the killer, but unfortunately a face is of no use without a name, except perhaps to Kojak or Dick Tracy.

The words floated from the tape machine like the sound of fingernails on a chalkboard.

"Well, here I am. I've got the funny money right here in the case. Let's see the real stuff."

Kelly had already decided there was no detectable accent. No use calling in dialect experts.

"Take it easy," he heard Rico say as the tape continued. "I've got the ten grand. . . . Look." Rico's voice was reassuring. He had learned the lesson well: always show confidence before the buy, to take the crook's mind off protecting himself. Makes him slower to react when the door goes down, gives the arrest team an edge.

Kelly heard the crinkling of the paper bag containing the buy money, then a "ping, ping" sound. Attaché case latches. He figured the case was probably opened on the bed, with the cover facing Rico so he couldn't see the sawed-off shotgun.

With the sound of the shotgun, Kelly crushed the empty plastic cup he was holding and slung it into a wastebasket.

"Turn it off for a second," Carr said with a wave of his hand.

Kelly slapped at the plastic buttons, and the tape stopped.

"There was no sound of a round being chambered or a safety being clicked off from the shotgun. That means it was ready to fire when he walked in the door. He didn't come to bluff. He intended to kill somebody."

Kelly nodded and turned on the machine again. By turning up the volume, they could hear the killer slam the case shut, run across the room, scramble out the window. Mixed with the sounds of the door being kicked in, they heard the killer's feet making crunching sounds as he ran down the gravel-covered driveway; then the sound of a car door, squealing tires.

"He must have cased the motel and seen the open window of room seven; otherwise he would have parked in the lot. It would have been easier," Kelly said.

"Wait a second," Carr interrupted. "Play it again. I think I've got something."

Kelly frowned as he snapped the cassette back in the machine. Listening to the tape made him sick to his stomach.

As the tape ran, Kelly noticed Carr looking at his watch. Finally, the tape ran out.

"He didn't start the engine," Carr said. "The sound of footsteps ended and the car zoomed off. The car door hadn't even closed."

"You're right," Kelly said. "He had to have had a getaway driver." Kelly wondered why he hadn't thought of that himself.

The wall phone rang, and Carr picked it up.

"Freddie Roth—are you sure? Okay, thanks."

Carr hung up the phone, walked to the workbench, and picked up the counterfeit ten-dollar bill.

"That was Delgado. A teletype just came in.

The D.C. lab says these tens are from an old Freddie Roth printing. It's the first time these particular notes have shown up in over five years."

"Now we have a lead," said Kelly.

$/4

Red Diamond sat on a barstool and sipped straight soda because it was easy on his stomach. The cocktail napkin under the soda read "The Paradise Isle—Hollywood's Friendliest Tavern," though to Red neither the five-foot-tall slimy-haired bartender not the two puffy-eyed bookies at the other end of the bar looked particularly friendly.

The place smelled like beer-soaked wood and wet ashes.

A wilted cartoon drawing of a giant-headed jockey (the bartender) astride a horse covered part of the spotty bar mirror. It was next to a chalkboard with scibbled messages. "The Commander—call Jimmy J." "Gloria—call your P.O." "Flaco—call the answering service in Vegas."

Red removed a half-dollar-size gambling chip from his pocket and tried to make it finger-walk on the back of his hand. The chip had inlaid red, white, and blue spots and bore a Sahara Club Casino camel trademark. He had discovered the chip in a satchel of personal belongings handed to him by a guard a half hour before he was released from Terminal Island. It had been nine days ago.

Obviously, he had overlooked the chip when he reported to the prison five years ealier to begin serving his sentence. Of course, in those days he considered a ten-spot as nothing more than toke money for the bellman, waiters, bartenders, and cocktail waitresses who had their mitts out when they saw him coming. That's the way it had been before everything went sour.

No period in his life had been more rewarding. For a while it seemed like the suckers had literally been *throwing* their money at him. . . . For once he had been accepted and protected by the big boys, and at home the Cherokee-blooded Mona had wrapped her velvety tippy-toe legs around him every night.

The prison stretch had certainly not been the first, but it had hurt more. Red attributed this to the age factor. After all, what in the world wasn't easier at twenty-five than at fifty-plus?

Red's sensitive colon gurgled. He restrained an urge to run for the men's room because he knew it was just nerves. Ronnie was an hour late. How long could it take to ditch a goddamn car?

The feeling in his bowels reminded him of the time he had posed as a bank courier and convinced a bank branch manager to give him three gold bars for delivery to Canada. As he stood in the bank's churchlike vault filling out the phony paperworks, he felt like he was going to mess his pants right then and there.

It had been mind over matter.

And mind over matter was why, at fifty-four years old, after serving five years flat for extortion, he was still able to come out fighting. He had slipped back five steps, but with a little luck, combined with good planning, he would soon be back in the running.

First he had to pay off Tony Dio, the loan shark.

During his first years in Terminal Island he had made himself believe that by the time he got out Dio would have died or something, and he would no longer owe the twenty-five grand. When he had borrowed it, he had had no problem paying the ten percent per week. Cash flow with the phony desert-land caper had been adequate to cover the nut. Then the rug was pulled out, and silk-tie Tony came to see him in the lockup and told him not to "worry" about paying it back until he got out of prison. Red had been out for nine days and he was worried. Maybe Ronnie's ten-grand score would keep Dio off his back for a while.

Right now, paying Dio back depended a lot on how well Ronnie performed. Ronnie had been useful in the federal pen. Anybody who's over fifty in the pen needed a bodyguard, and Ronnie had benefited by learning about something other than lowbrow, chickenshit bank jobs.

Red looked at his watch again, and scratched his balding pate fiercely. Much of the hair on top had fallen out during the last stretch, though the sides were still red and frizzy. He ordered another straight soda.

The bartender washed glasses. "I've seen you before," he said. His facial features were small, rodentlike, except for a set of oversized, improperly spaced teeth. He wore a long-sleeved polka-dot shirt with underarm stains.

"Think so?"

"Yep. You used to be with Tony Dio a few years back. I was tending bar at the Crossroads in Beverly Hills. You and him used to come in all the time. You guys were always buying rounds."

So big fucking deal, thought Red. "Small world," he said, looking at his watch. Ronnie, where are you?, he said to himself.

The little man filled a glass with ice, poured soda, and placed it gently next to Red's half-full drink. His fingernails were dirty. "I remembered because of the soda. You always ordered straight soda. I never forget a drink. . . . Name's Gabe." He hesitated a moment before sticking out his hand. "You probably remember me."

They shook hands. As Red had feared, the handshake suddenly made things chummy. Gabe rested his elbows on the bar and leaned close to Red's face.

He whispered, "I figure you must have just got out. I remember the case in the papers. Five years ago. It took the bank months to figure out what had happened. What was it? Phony bank loans to get stocks?"

Red shook his head. "Phony stocks to get bank loans."

"Yeah." The bartender beamed. "How did it work?"

"Too complicated to explain." Red looked at his watch again.

"I'm glad to see classy dudes like yourself in here. You ain't got no worries in here. I know most everybody that comes in. What goes down in here stays here. No turkeys in this crowd." He wiped his hands on the front of his pants.

Gabe shuffled to the end of the bar and served drinks to some bookmakers who had been alternately using the phone in the men's room. He hurried back to his old buddy.

Red cringed.

"Tony Dio's *big* now. *Real* big," Gabe said. "He can get *anything* done."

"That's what I hear," Red said.

Ronnie Boyce walked in the door in a blast of acrid L.A. heat, and Red's entire stomach felt better immediately. He motioned to Ronnie with both hands.

"What took so damn long? I thought you got popped or something. *Jesus!*"

Ronnie sat down on a barstool. "Couldn't find a bus back. I parked it down on Central Avenue. When the cops find it, they'll figure some nigger stole it." He motioned to the bartender.

"Very good. Very good," said Red. He removed a ball-point pen from his pocket and wrote on a cocktail napkin "Recovery operation."

"I'm proud of you, little brother. Stage one is complete," he said. "We're ahead of the game by ten grand. I want you to keep two grand for yourself right off the top. Buy yourself some clothes or something." He spoke as earnestly as possible, not sure if even dumb-as-a-rabbit Ronnie would buy what he said.

"I'll need the rest to start setting up the 'front.' Just like we talked about in the joint. These things take money. For a successful project we'll need a dummy office in Century City or on Wilshire Boulevard—and that takes *money*. You know that. Put the bucks in to get the bucks out. The suckers are out there just waiting. Right, partner?" Red put his arm around Ronnie's shoulder, waiting for a reaction. Ronnie nodded.

Red continued, speaking briskly. "With the getaway and everthing, I still haven't got the exact details. I want you to relax and tell me just what happened in the room. After a caper it always pays to check for loose ends."

Ronnie's voice was youthful, soft. "I knocked on the door; he let me in. He was alone. Everything went pretty much just like you told me it would. He shows me the buy money, then I set my case on the bed between me and his. I whip out the sawed-off and let loose. You should have seen it. He flew back all the way across the room. And you know something? When he went down, I saw that he had an ankle gun on. If I wouldn't have done him, he might have done me, right?" Ronnie tapped his chest with his thumb.

Red swallowed hard. "You did exactly the right thing. You just made the big time. I'm proud of you, little brother. Your old Red buddy is proud."

Ronnie smiled broadly. "It really worked, just like you said it would."

Red patted his arm. "And the best part is that there isn't going to be any heat from the cops. When the cops find a stiff in a motel room, the first thing they do is run fingerprints. When they do that, they see that the dude has an arrest sheet. The first thing cops figure is that it was nothing but a thieves' argument and they close the case. That's as far as they go. See, I know how the pigs think. I used to have a lot of 'em drinking in my place in Long Beach in the old days. I used to hear 'em talk when they didn't think nobody was listening. You see, they actually *like* to find a dead thief. They get off on that kind of shit. And that's no lie. That's how they are. To them a dead thief is just less work."

Ronnie nodded his head without speaking, an athlete listening to the coach after competition.

Red continued. "I want you to take the sawed-off and stash it like I explained, and then enjoy yourself for a couple of days. Go see your old girlfriend like you been talking about. Why don't you meet me here day after tomorrow and I'll fill you in on stage two. As soon as we have enough capital, we'll be able to pull one big con and we'll be set for life, partner." The words flowed easily for Red. It was the same thing he had been telling Ronnie in stir for years, though Red knew that the last thing he would ever do would be to get involved in a confidence caper again. He was well known by the Feds and bunco cops from Hollywood to Fort Lauderdale. Christ, how many confidence men had red hair?

Red was too old to get his own hands dirty and end up doing another stretch.

$15

On the way to the hotel Red Diamond drove past
the glass-and-steel high-rise buildings in L.A.'s
Century City: twenty-story condominium struc-
tures and plushly carpeted office suites for rent or
lease. This is where I belong, thought Red. My
milieu. He knew that with a few bucks he could
rent an office in one of the high-rises again. He
could start putting people on "hold" by pushing
the lighted buttons on the phone. "Hold, please,
for Mr. Diamond," the secretary had said. The
high-rise world was a mystery to the pussy-headed
group counselors at Terminal Island. "Inflated
self-image," one had called it. "Don't you think
your schemes could relate to your childhood con-
flicts?" the counselor had asked him.

Red remembered how he had slowly, carefully,
over the period of a full year of tedious prison-
counseling sessions, faked coming around to the
counselor's point of view. It had been sort of a chal-
lenge, not to mention that there was nothing else
to do. The pussy-headed dollar-an-hour dumb bastard finally bought his rehabilitation act and at
the end of the year gave him a progress rating

high enough for parole consideration. The counselor had taken the hook and swallowed it because he was like every other sucker in the world—prone to accept his own fantasy and susceptible to flattery. Red's credo proved true again.

Imagine, Red thought, a two-bit Department of Prisons civil servant with two semesters of psychology writing a report on the behavior of Mr. Rudolph Diamond, former president of Gold Futures Unlimited, Sun King Recreational Properties Corporation, and the International Investment Bank of Nassau, in the Bahamas, whose buxom young secretary used to blow him as he leaned back on the Danish modern sofa in his office at the Century Building.

Red pulled up in front of the multistoried hotel and handed the car keys to a doorman dressed like a caballero.

He took a deep breath and knocked on the suite door. He was conscious of dampness in his armpits.

The door was opened quickly, chain still on, by a husky man in a flowered shirt. Red noticed a gun bulge at the man's waist.

"I have an appointment with Tony Dio," Red said.

The man unlatched the chain and ushered him over plush, thick carpet to a small balcony. On the balcony, without a word, the man began to frisk him. Ignoring this, Red sat down at the balcony table. He faced the ocean.

"Hey, I'm not finished patting you down, pal."

"Where's Tony?"

"You ain't going to see him until I see if you are wired up, pal."

"Tell Tony he can search me himself if he thinks I'm a snitch. Keep your goddamn hands off me." Red stared at the ocean.

Tony Dio, in a tennis outfit and smoked glasses, walked onto the balcony and flicked his cigar ashes over the rail. He looked as if he had been gaining weight for the past five years—King Farouk in tennis shorts. He did not shake hands.

The man in the flowered shirt walked back inside.

Dio turned and looked down at Red.

"Don't let him bother you. He does that to everybody. You know how things are these days." He stuck the cigar in his mouth.

"All I need is another couple of months," Red said. "I have a project planned and I just need a little time. I'm trying to get back on my feet. You know that."

Dio puffed and blew smoke into the breeze. He did not look at Red.

"Red, in the old days, when we were just little guys, there was no quibbling about a few bucks here or there. It's different now. It's all points, you know, *percentages*. Everything is points and deadlines."

The veins on Red's neck stood out. He clenched his fists.

"I just did a nickel in Terminal Island. I'm fifty-four years old. This is it for me. This is my last shot. I've got a big project planned. When it comes through I'll be able to pay you off with interest for the whole five years. You know I'm good for the twenty-five grand."

Dio turned to him and took the cigar from his mouth. "I know you are good for it. That's why I

let the debt ride while you were in the joint. . . .
Now you are out. I placed my bet on the 'come
line.' " He stared.

Red felt sweat begin to run from his armpits to
his waist.

"I wasn't born yesterday," he said. "All I'm asking is more time. I guarantee that I'll . . ."

"How much did you bring with you today?"
Dio interrupted.

"Eight grand." Red laid the envelope on the table.

"Take your time with the rest," Dio said. He
gazed at the ocean again. "Take another ten
days."

Red stood up. "How about thirty days? I mean,
there's always last-minute problems. . . ."

"Thanks for stopping by, Red," Dio said.

As Red walked through the living room to the
door the man in the flowered shirt stood behind a
portable bar, watching. Red wondered if he would
be the one to get the contract if he couldn't come
up with the money.

In the hallway, waiting for the elevator, Red
recognized the falling-away feeling, with its con-
comitant fire in the intestinal tract. He had made
notes about the feeling in his cell and had reread
them often. The name falling-away feeling was
coined by him because "falling away" was the
opposite of things "going one's way," that is, goals
being reached, predictions of success coming
true . . . big scores.

Red's notes had reflected that the feeling
usually, but not always, was present shortly before
a disaster, when things started to get out of control. A sucker screams about his money and calls

the cops; shortly thereafter handcuffs bite the wrists. Even psychiatrists, actual doctors of the mind, could not predict human behavior one hundred percent of the time.

The falling-away feeling was a signal calling for careful planning to find the way out. And Red knew that there was, in every bad situation, a *way* out. Patience was required. And occasionally (he remembered specifically writing this with an exclamation point in a margin) brute force. In other words, "God helps those who help themselves."

The elevator doors opened soundlessly for Red Diamond. He stepped in and they closed. "The primary objective is to reduce risk," he said out loud.

Ronnie Boyce removed the fancy pink package from the attaché case and placed it in the rental locker. After glancing at the passengers in the bus terminal, he closed the locker quickly, removed the key, and pushed it into the pocket of his leather jacket.

On the way from Red's, he had bought birthday paper and wrapped the sawed-off shotgun. Red had told him it was the best precaution against a general inspection of such lockers. He said they usually wouldn't go to the trouble of opening a gift-wrapped package. Happy birthday, mother fuckers, he thought.

Before meeting Red, he would never have gone to such trouble. Now such precautions were a source of pride. "No bull can prove a murder case without the murder weapon," Red often said.

It was dusk when Ronnie drove toward the Sea Horse Motel. He left the Santa Monica Freeway and headed south on Lincloln Boulevard and smelled salt air. The smell reminded him of Carol's beach apartment six years ago. He pictured her walking around the apartment naked, tits jiggling, talking a hundred miles an hour. He thought of the arrow tattoo.

At a traffic light, a woman in tennis shorts crossed the street in snappy fashion. Her legs were long, like Carol's. Although he remembered Carol's body, he wasn't sure he would remember her face. He had not seen her since the trial, six years ago. She had sat in the dock like a penguin and testified against him. For the first months in stir he had dreamed of escaping just to kill her, but those thoughts had faded into others. Walking the yard was a mind bender.

He knew it had been his fault. After all, he chose to live with her and let her in on the bank jobs. What the hell did he expect her to do? Carol would never ride a beef for a man. She was a loner. She was one of the few broads who had her own reputation. Carol was the Queen of Plastic. She could have written books on how to make two grand a day from a hot American Express card.

He swung into the lot in front of a row of aqua-colored motel rooms and parked. He checked the note in his wallet. Sea Horse, room eleven. She had been easy to locate through the grapevine.

He walked to room eleven and knocked loudly. There was no answer. After looking around, he removed the screwdriver from his pocket, jimmied the lock, opened the door, and stepped into the darkened room. Women's clothes lay on the bed; a brassiere hung on a chair. Closing the door, he moved a chair to a corner of the room and sat on it.

He removed the switch-blade knife from his pocket, flicked it open, and cleaned his nails. The motel room was fairly clean, but small, cell-like. A print of an ocean scene hung over the bed. The room reminded him of the Burbank apartment where he had played as a child. Walls thin as paper. His mother had liked the apartment because it was near the studios, where she had worked on and off as a waitress. He remembered the cheap furniture and the hundreds of tiny bottles and jars on her dressing table, the *Screen Romance* magazines in the kitchen drawer, the enormous photo of Alan Ladd on the living-room wall, the smell of cold cream.

He had spent the first night away from the apartment in Los Angeles County Juvenile Hall. The next day, good old Mom had come to pick him up, carting along a whiskey-breath boyfriend. They dropped him off at the apartment after she scolded him for breaking into a car. She hadn't even taken the trouble to find out that he had broken into a house, not a car.

He had received a telegram about her death when he was in Chino serving three years for some gas-station stickups. After learning the news, he had finished his handball game.

He heard a key enter the lock and he stood up quietly with the knife in his hand.

She did not see him as she closed the door and walked to the dressing table. She turned on the table lamp; her back was to him but she saw him in the mirror and gave a sharp cry. Her hands flew to her mouth and she spun around. They faced each other across the messy bed.

"Ronnie! Oh! Please don't kill me. The Feds made me testify. I didn't want to. They tricked me. Oh, God. NO!" Her knees and thighs were held stiffly together.

He noticed the crow's-feet and the extremely short bleached hair. Her voice was the same, deep, almost hoarse. She wore jeans and a silk blouse.

"I guess you know that I woulda never got convicted if you wouldn't have testified." He held the knife loosely in his right hand.

"I just got out a month ago myself. . . . What . . . are you going to do? What are you going to do to me?"

"I was going to choke you to death. Or maybe just cut off your tongue."

Her fists clenched. After a moment of silence she began speaking, her voice shrill, staccato. "I want you to do it," she babbled, "I want you to kill me right now. I want to get it over with. I deserve it for being a snitch. You were my baby and I snitched. I wanted to write you and tell you what happened but I knew you wouldn't understand. . . ."

"Carol, don't try to con me. You're not talking to some bank turkey to set up a phony account. You're talking to Ronnie Boyce. And I'll tell you right off I'm six years smarter than I ever was. I'm *together* this time: one-hundred-fucking-percent *together*."

She fell silent as he spoke, but glanced toward the door.

"Don't look at the door, woman. You ain't going

nowhere." Ronnie sat down nonchalantly on the chair. It seemed that they had been staring at each other for hours.

"I heard you ended up in Corona three years ago. I guess you didn't have anybody to snitch off on that case."

With a moan, Carol sat down on the edge of the bed, hands over her eyes and forehead.

"You were all I thought about the whole thirty months," she sobbed, looking up, then covering her eyes again quickly.

Ronnie was quiet for what must have been ten minutes. "Don't get the idea that you've conned me, Carol," he said at last. "Nobody does that to me. If I came here to ice you, that's just what I would have done."

She looked up.

"I just want to make it up to you," she said softly. Her chest was heaving, thrusting, under the silk blouse. Her eyes were piercing.

Ronnie did not answer immediately. Perhaps without admitting it, he had known all along he wanted her back. In prison, his mind had allowed her many fates. Now that he really was finally out, the choice was either to snuff her because of what she had done or to let her live and have things like they were.

He put the blade of the knife back in the handle and tossed it across the bed into her lap. She looked up, startled.

"I'll make it up to you. Everything will be okay again," she said.

"The only way you could make it up to me would be to go down on it nonstop for six god-damn years." His voice was sad.

51

She smiled cautiously, stood up, and stripped quickly, efficiently, jabbering away as if nothing had happened, as if the six years had been six days.

No reason to kill her now, he thought, it wouldn't prove anything.

Naked, she walked around the bed and faced him. He stared at the tattooed arrow on the thigh pointing upward toward the hair. Christ, in how many prison dreams had he seen the tattoo? Once, he had drawn the arrow on a photo in *Playboy*.

"I ain't going to go back," he said.

Quickly, she dropped to her knees in front of him. "Everything's going to be okay again. Come here now, let me see . . ." said Carol, reaching for him. He grasped the sides of her head.

$16

The federal prison was located on the south end of Terminal Island, the gun tower being positioned next to sea rocks. The prison itself was separated from the steam-belching canneries on the island by various perimeters of chain-link topped with barbed wire. The canneries and dead seaweed along the rocks gave the whole place the smell of rotten eggs.

In the prison's parking lot, Charles Carr locked his gun and handcuffs in the trunk of the government sedan and headed for the two-story administration building. The drab brownstone structure accented a steel door with reinforced hinges. It was the only way in and out.

Inside the building he displayed his badge, signed the visitor's register, and filled out two useless forms.

In an interview room, he reviewed Freddie Roth's lengthy prison file, concentrating on the latest stretch.

Carr remembered his first meeting with Freddie Roth. The door of the print shop had gone down. Freddie was back-pedaling past the press with greenish hands in the air. "Okay. You got me. You got me."

Inside the print shop Carr had holstered his gun and bantered with Freddie for over an hour about where he had hidden the plates. "On my mother's grave," chanted Freddie, "I destroyed 'em. Go ahead and look! Be my guest. You won't find any plates. I burned 'em with a blowtorch and dumped 'em in the ocean. So help me God!"

And there was the blank look on Roth's face when the plates were pulled out of the floor safe—not a smile or a frown, just a business-as-usual, do-my-time, see-you-when-I-get-out-again expression.

The interview room was neat. Two chairs, a table, a tiny aluminum-foil ashtray. The walls were freshly painted light green. The paint odor combined with a hangover caused Carr to feel slightly light-headed. He wished he had eaten breakfast.

He stopped turning the pages of Roth's prison file and looked up. The khaki-uniformed guard stepped in the door carrying a steaming mug of coffee. Carr noticed tattoos on his giant arms, a full head of thick hair combed backward with grease.

"You Carr? Treasury?"

Carr nodded. "I'm waiting for Roth to be brought down from D wing . . . Frederick Roth."

After another loud slurp, which caused Carr to stifle a gag, the guard leaned forward for coffee-breath emphasis. "Before you talk to him, there's something you may want to know. He's been in my office begging for a gate pass for the past month. The pass would allow him to be assigned

54

to the work detail in the minimum-security wing. I was going to approve the pass until I found out about his old lady."

"His old lady?" Carr looked puzzled.

"She wrote him a Dear John last month. We read all the letters coming in. The bleeding hearts haven't taken that away from us yet. Seems she moved in with a colored gentleman since poor old Freddie's been in barbwire city. Freddie tried to smuggle a letter out to her." The guard dug into his shirt pocket. "Here's a copy of it."

Carr read the letter as the guard lapped at the mug.

The last line of the letter read, "I'll be getting out of here sooner than you think, bitch. Then you and your nigger are going to die."

"The reason he's pushing for a gate pass is that the minimum-security wing gives him access to the highway. It's the easiest way to escape. You can rest assured the last thing he will *ever* get is a gate pass." The guard smiled wryly.

With the knock on the door, Carr handed the letter back, and the guard quickly stuffed it in his pants pocket. The guard stood up and motioned Roth to the table, stepped outside, and closed the door. Carr heard the snap of the lock.

A gaunt Freddie Roth sat down and gushed insincere greetings about how pleased he was to see the "old fox." Roth's bald head and his face appeared yellow, cadaverous, just as Carr remembered them. His glasses were much thicker.

"This place is a little different from my pad in Malibu years ago, eh? Remember?" Roth motioned to the green walls as if introducing a choir. "It is really good to see yez. Really, I'm very serious about it. It really is good to see yez." He spoke as if he were selling a vacuum cleaner.

"Got a date yet, Freddie?"

"I was supposed to have a date by now, but they turned over my house during a lockdown and found some seed, so they held up my date. The grass wasn't even mine. . . . What do you want to talk to me about?" He pushed his glasses back on his nose.

"Some of your old twenties have been showing up recently," Carr said.

Roth leaned forward, interested, elbows on knees. The glasses slipped again.

"Which old twenties?"

"The ones you printed just before this stretch."

Roth rubbed a hand across the desert of his scalp. "Yes, the plate had a bad key in the Treasury seal." He shook his head. "I should have burned the whole friggin' batch instead of putting them out on the street. I'm almost embarrassed to say they were my work."

"Santa Anita and Hollywood Park didn't think they were so bad," Carr said.

Roth beamed. "The casinos in Las Vegas put out a notice on them, too, as a matter of fact. I had a friend there who checked for me. . . . I was peddling them for *thirty* points on the dollar. *Six bucks* apiece. And even with that price, my phone was ringing off the hook."

"Who has the rest of the notes, Freddie?" Carr's tone was fatherly.

Roth held out his hands. "Wait a minute! Did you come here to lay a goddamn case on me while I'm in the joint? What the hell do I know about who has a few twenties that I printed three years ago? How do *I* know what's happening on the street right now? I'm in a *cage*, man. I . . ."

"Thanks, Freddie," Carr interrupted. "You can go now. Sorry to bother you."

Roth's yellow jaw dropped. "What?"

"I said you can go back to D wing. I don't have any more questions," Carr said. Through the years Carr had learned that Roth had to be kept on the track.

Roth slid his chair back to stand up. He stopped.

"What if I *was* to remember something about a stash on the outside. What's in it for me?" He sat down again.

"What do you *want* to be in it for you?" Carr said.

Roth put his hands in his lap. "It's like this. I'm on the list to get a gate pass to minimum security so I can work outside on the grass. I'm sick and I need some sun and fresh air; vitamin C. You know how it is. . . . If you could talk to the captain and move my name up on the gate-pass list, I think I might be able to remember something about the twenties. Get the picture?"

"I get the picture," Carr said. "I'll go see the guard captain and see what I can do."

Carr stood up and knocked on the door. A guard unlocked and opened it. He stepped out into the shiny corridor and walked toward the prison-staff coffee room. As he walked he noticed the yellow that was building up along the baseboards. Unnecessary waxing, like the cheap labor of an army headquarters company.

In the empty coffee room, Carr picked up a

well-worn copy of the *Los Angeles Times*. He read halfway through a feature article on how a small town in Ohio had lowered the crime rate by arresting all its heroin addicts. He thought of one apartment house near McArthur Park where at least fifty addicts lived. The addicts in that apartment house alone would fill up most smalltown jails. He threw the paper down.

Leaning back on the sofa, he thought of the smelly Quonset hut outside Seoul where he first practiced real-life interrogation. The methods were different then, but the motivations the same. It was simply a matter of finding the right chord and playing it no holds barred. Carr closed his eyes.

A half hour later, he got up from the sofa, returned to the interview room, and sat down. He looked Roth directly in the eye.

"It looks like you are in luck. I had to take a lot of jaw from the captain, but he finally agreed to go along with the gate pass if I tell him you cooperated with me fully. The deal is on." Carr continued to peer into the other's eyes, for a sincere effect.

"How do I know you're tellin' me the truth?" Roth said. Using his index finger he made a figure-eight pattern on the table top.

Carr stared at the floor for a moment, then spoke clearly and loudly. "I just went in and made a fool out of myself making a deal for you, clown. Either give me the story right now or you go back to your cell, and I'll be on my way. I don't like people who waste my time. I'm tired of this stinking room. I have a hangover. Fuck you."

Carr stood up, knocking his chair back violently, and walked toward the door.

"Okay," Roth said. "Sit down and I'll tell you the whole thing. But I better not be ripped off. If anybody finds out I'm helping the Feds, I could end up getting shanked. There's guys in here that actually *like* to do it. . . ."

"So I've heard," Carr interrupted. "Who's holding your stash?"

"I don't want to get anybody involved. I gave my stash to a friend to hold for me. He's got about fifty grand. It was left over from the printing. You guys missed it when you broke down the door. I had it buried two blocks away." Roth cleaned his glasses on his shirttail.

"What is your friend's name?"

Roth put his glasses back on. "This guy is a real friend, man. I don't want to see him drop behind a deal where he was just doing me a favor. You know what I mean?"

"How bad do you want the gate pass?" Carr asked.

Roth closed his eyes, opened them, then spoke. "Virgil Leach. He deals in paper. You can find him at the Paradise Isle in Hollywood. He's called 'Pleach.' That's a combination of 'pimple' and 'leach.' You'll know why when you see him. Gotta girlfriend named Vikki; she has a big habit. Now you know as much as I do."

"Why is Leach holding your stash?"

"He's just a friend, a paper passer from the old days. After you guys busted me I knew there would be heat on the serial numbers. I asked him to hold the stuff for me until I got out of the joint.

I wasn't going to pass any. I just didn't know what to do with them." His expression was somber.

Carr nodded, as if he understood. He stood up to leave.

"When do I get my gate pass?" Roth said.

"Just as soon as it's typed up." Carr knocked on the door. It was opened. He stepped into the hallway and told the guard to take the prisoner back to his cell.

$17

It was dark.

Carr looked through the binoculars at Virgil Leach's small wood-framed house. It was nestled next to a modern-looking, pink stucco apartment house. A Cadillac was parked in the driveway. Except for the apartment house, the neighborhood was run down; property values on the decline. "Urban decay," as *Time* would say.

Kelly dozed at the wheel.

After stopping by the state parole office to pick up Leach's mug photo and current address, they had driven directly to Leach's house and begun the surveillance. It had been a long day.

Carr put the binoculars back in the glove compartment. Out of boredom he picked up the Xerox copies of the parole reports again. Leach's mug shot was stapled to the first page. Carr thought of the "before" photograph in an acne-medicine ad.

Leach was described in the reports as a forty-year-old with a "sociopathic personality with emotional blunting."

Kelly yawned loudly and began rubbing his eyes. "You still reading that bullshit?" he said.

"I thought it was more interesting than listening to your snore."

"Man, am I hungry." Kelly rubbed his stomach.

"So what else is new?" Carr smiled, lifting the binoculars to his eyes again. He adjusted the lens.

"I got my evaluation today. No Waves put it in on my desk so he wouldn't have to face me. It was a 'sandwich job' as usual."

"A what?"

Kelly reached into his inside coat pocket and took out a typed Special Agent Yearly Evaluation Form. "Listen to this," he said. "Special Agent Kelly is an experienced senior agent who can be counted upon to fulfill his responsibilities. He is an excellent marksman and has a high record of arrests and convictions. At times his outspokenness causes problems with his coworkers. Kelly has a thorough knowledge of the operations manual and keeps his reports up to date." Kelly folded the paper and stuffed it back in his coat pocket. "See? A sandwich job. He starts with good points, then the bad, then ends with something good. A shit sandwich. Just enough to keep me from getting promoted, but not enough to get me pissed off . . . What did he put in yours this time?"

"Same as yours, except for the bad part. Mine said something like 'Carr has a tendency to be too independent. He objects to proper supervision and has on occasion refused to indentify his informants when told to do so.'"

"Good old No Waves. He wouldn't know an informant if one bit him on the ass. The pipe-smoking, briefcase-carrying, ass-licking, back-stabbing prick. Did I ever tell you about the time he interviewed me on a brutality allegation?"

Carr shook his head no even though he knew the story by heart.

"He sits there behind his desk with two inspectors in the room, tape recorder on. The interview was almost over, and he says, 'Well, you know how it is. We have to follow up on rumors.' I said, 'I hear rumors every day.' He said, 'Like what?' So I said, 'Yesterday somebody told me you were a queer.' The friggin' inspectors almost fell off their chairs!" Kelly laughed furiously, caught his breath, and laughed again.

Leach walked from his front door. He wore European-cut trousers that were too small for his chunky frame, and a waist-length leather jacket that would have looked good on a nineteen-year-old.

"Okay. We've finally got some movement," Carr said.

Kelly rubbed his face roughly with both hands and started the engine.

Leach got into the Cadillac. The headlights came on. He backed out of the driveway and pulled into traffic.

Kelly, without headlights, kept at a safe distance behind the Cadillac as it drove along shabby side streets toward Wilshire Boulevard. Carr wished Leach would get onto a larger street so the tandem turns would not be so obvious.

The Cadillac turned west on Wilshire Boulevard.

Carr thought they had lost him for a moment when he made a left turn on Vermont. They caught up to the Cadillac as it entered the freeway. The trip to Marina Del Rey was easy because there were a million cars on the freeway. Carr knew that all headlights would look the same in Leach's rearview mirror; an easy tail.

As Leach pulled into a valet lot at the Captain's Disco he almost ran into a bevy of sun-tanned young women dressed in jeans and tank tops. He got out of his car and handed the keys to the valet. He walked up the steps and in the front door.

"Everybody here is either a pipe smoker or a stewardess," Kelly said. "If Leach brought a pipe, he should fit right in."

"You take the point," Carr said. "I'll wait here."

Kelly took off his suit coat and gun and threw them on the back seat. He trotted up the steps, paid his cover charge at the door, and went in. Carr could hear the faint echo of rock music.

Waiting, Carr turned on the radio and listened to a late-night talk program. The disc jockey's voice sounded bored, sleepy, as he discussed capital punishment with a shut-in who kept coughing. They used the word *deterrent* over and over again. Carr leaned back in the seat.

It was 1:30 A.M. when Kelly came back out. He waved to Carr and headed for a phone booth in the parking lot next door. The phone call was brief.

After Kelly hung up the phone, it was exactly four minutes until a black-and-white police car drove into the parking lot.

Kelly approached it. The uniformed officers inside nodded their heads as Kelly displayed his Treasury badge. After speaking animatedly for a few moments, he pointed toward Leach's Cadillac. After a short discussion, the police car pulled out of the lot and parked down the street.

Kelly trotted back to the car and slid into the driver's seat. He turned off the radio.

"He's ready," he told Carr. "I counted at least seven drinks. He's in there trying to pick up teeny-boppers, but they've all shined him on."

Leach walked out the front door and waited for the valet to bring the Cadillac. He looked unsteady on his feet. He seemed to fall into his car as the valet opened the door.

The red lights of the police car went on as soon as the Cadillac passed.

Kelly started the engine. They drove past the flashing red light of the police car and saw Leach, arms outstretched, trying to touch the tip of his index finger to his pimpled nose.

Kelly stepped on the gas.

The black sheriff's deputy shoved Leach roughly into the dark cell.

Carr lay on the top bunk feigning sleep, his face embedded in a pillow that smelled faintly of Clorox. He had decided not to say anything until morning, figuring that Leach would not be too enthusiastic about gabbing with a cellmate at 3:00 A.M. No use rushing it.

Leach walked the four steps to the commode and urinated loudly. He flopped on the lower bunk and dropped his shoes to the floor one at a time. He began snoring within ten minutes.

Carr told himself there was no reason why he shouldn't be able to sleep. He rethought the tack he would use, then dozed fitfully.

An echoing scream woke him. He sat up in the bunk. There was the sound of a scuffle farther down the tier, then a loud moaning. People fighting over a cigarette or perhaps a plastic comb?

Carr rolled over and stared at the flaking ceiling. He thought of bicycling along the beach to Sally's house; he knocked and she wasn't home. He closed his eyes.

Carr woke up as the tier lights went on. He slid off the bunk, put his shoes on, and washed his face with cold water at the yellowish sink. The cell reminded him of a service-station bathroom: filthy cement.

"How long you been in?" asked Leach, yawning. He stood up from the bunk, stretching. He had no shirt on. His face was a mask of ripe, red infections, his neck a collar of thick purple scar tissue with protruding unshavable whiskers.

"Ten days," Carr answered. He dried his hands on a gray towel.

"What're you in for?" Leach yawned again without covering his mouth.

"Drunk driving," Carr said. "I'm getting out today." ("Chance meetings require common topics," said the agents' manual.)

"No shit," Leach said. "That's what I'm in for. Had a few drinks at a bar. I'm on my way home and the cops give me the red light. No shit." He made his fingers into a comb and raked his sticky hair.

"The goddamn pigs must of needed one more for their quota," Carr said. Without looking at the other man, he climbed back onto the top bunk, lit a cigarette, and leaned against the wall.

Leach was at the sink now, drinking handfuls from the faucet. He spit water into the sink.

"Sounds like you don't get along with the man." Leach looked at his wet hands for a moment, turned, and began drying them on a corner of Carr's blanket.

"Get your hands off the blanket," Carr said matter-of-factly.

Leach stopped drying his hands with the blanket but continued to hold it. He stared amusedly at Carr. "Sounds like you learned some of the rules during the last ten days."

"I learned the rules in Leavenworth," Carr said. "Now get your goddamn hooks off the blanket." ("Don't be afraid to poke the lion," said the T-school instructor.)

Leach dropped the corner of the blanket. "No shit," he said. "How much time did you do in Leavenworth?" He rubbed his hands back and forth on his pants.

"A deuce."

"What for?"

"Passing funny money," Carr said.

"No shit? How'd they make you on it?"

"Feds lied on me in court. Said they found funny money in my car." He paused. "What makes you so interested?"

Leach opened up his palms and furrowed his brow. "Easy, dude! You're talking to somebody who's done time in *Folsom, Atlanta,* and *San Quentin.* Maybe you heard of me. Papers used to call me 'The Drugstore Forger.' I was in the papers and everything before my last case. Name's Leach. They call me 'Pleach.' " He stuck out his hand for the jive handshake.

"Right on," Carr said. He shook hands.

Carr smelled the odor of oatmeal and grease as

67

it wafted along the cell block, mixing with that of humans in cages of concrete. A cement nursery school?

Leach stepped to the bars and grasped them. "My bail bondsman should be waiting in the arraignment court to bail me out," he said.

"I should make the noon release myself. This is my last day." Carr bit his lip, hoping Leach would take the bait.

"No shit."

That was the last thing Leach said for a few minutes.

Finally he spoke. "What do you have planned?"

"Make a few bucks and head back east," Carr said.

"I'm going to pick up some phony cashier's checks soon as I get out. A friend's got a load. They're always easy to down without ID."

"Not as easy as funny money."

"Maybe not, but he ain't got funny money. He's got checks."

"Who's your friend?" He cupped his hand to his ear. "Speak up. I didn't hear you."

"Just testing," said the scarred man.

Nothing more was said for at least a half hour.

"Are you still into funny money?" Leach said at last.

Carr casually swung his feet over the side of the bunk. "You might say that."

$/8

Carr heard the sheriff's deputies walking along the tier as they called out prisoners' names. "Bloodsaw, Tyrone. Zavala, Jesus. Leach, Virgil."

"Here!" Leach answered. The deputy stepped to the bars, checked Leach's wrist tag. "Courtline bus number one," the deputy said, looking at a clipboard.

"Looks like I'll be bailed out in an hour or so. I got the first bus. . . . By the way, what's your name?"

"Charlie."

Leach eyed the deputy. He whispered, "Charlie, think you'd be interested in some nice green stuff? No shit."

"What flavor?" Carr said.

"Number twenty . . . with ten different serial numbers." He held up all fingers.

"What's the price?"

"Eighteen points on the dollar. A hundred and eighty bucks for a grand."

The hydraulic lock snapped open cells farther down the tier. Prisoners shuffled.

"I might be interested."

"No shit. How much can you handle?"

"How much heat is on the batch?" Carr said. "Are the Feds on to the serial numbers?"

"No way, my man. The product is cool. No shit. If you can prove otherwise, I'll give you your money back . . . and that is no shit." Leach stuffed cigarettes in his pocket. He tucked in his prison shirt.

The hydraulic lock buzzed, and the cell door slid open slowly. "You'll make the noon release, right?" Leach said.

Carr nodded.

Leach whispered from the side of his mouth. "Meet me tonight at the Paradise Isle on Hollywood Boulevard. I'll have a sample for you. No shit." He stepped out of the cell.

Carr waited on a barstool at the Paradise Isle. The place was dark and crowded, the jukebox deafening. Kelly sat at the opposite end of the bar, near the rear door. He wore a purple bowling shirt and needed a shave.

Carr felt uneasy. The place was all nicknames and handshakes. A fat blonde touched tongues with the black man next to her, knocking off his knit cap.

"Haven't seen ya here before," the bartender said. "Name's Gabe."

Carr shook the offered wet hand.

"Waiting for somebody?"

"Pleach. You seen him around?"

"He'll be in. Stops by every night. Nuther drink?" A fish smile.

Carr nodded.

Gabe served Carr another drink. He dried

glasses for a few minutes before approaching Kelly, the other stranger in the place. He asked the preliminaries.

"I'm waiting for some good-looking cunt to walk in here. That's what I'm waiting for," Kelly said, in his normal tone of voice. The fat blonde looked up.

Gabe offered his hand to the Irishman. Kelly put his glass in it. "Put some booze in it this time, little man."

Gabe frowned.

Carr sipped his drink, wondering whether he and Kelly had passed the bartender's test.

Gabe picked up the phone at the end of the bar and dialed, whispered a few words, and hung up.

Fifteen minutes later Leach came in the back door and walked directly to the bar. Carr's breathing quickened.

"See? I showed up," said Leach. "No shit."

"That's good. I don't like to be hung up."

"Don't worry about Pleach. I always take care of business." He swung himself onto a barstool.

"We gonna be able to do some business tonight?" Carr asked.

"That depends." Leach glanced at the black wearing the knit cap. "After I bailed out today I started thinking. I don't know you. Nothing personal, you understand. I just don't know where you're comin' from. I mean like I just met you in County last night and I really haven't had time to check you out. No shit."

The bartender handed Leach a drink. He took a sip.

"In other words, you were just running your mouth this morning and you don't really have a

71

connection. Is that what you're telling me?" Carr smiled.

"No, I didn't say that." Leach smiled back.

"Because if it is, it's no problem. I just talked to another guy today who's got some paper lined up for me. Fifties, with all different serial numbers. Price isn't as good as yours, but he'll come down. What I'm saying is that I can score tonight somewhere else." Carr took a sip and placed the glass back on the wet napkin.

"Oh," Leach said. He picked at his face for a moment, then stopped abruptly. "What if I said I could get you a load tonight? Do you have the four grand right now?"

"Sure. I got the four G's right here in my pocket. I'm sitting here in this toilet with my back facing the door and I've got four grand in my pocket. I'm tired of living. I *want* to get ripped off."

"I don't mean *that*. I mean can you come up with the money tonight if I can get . . ."

Carr leaned over and spoke directly into the other's face. "What did I tell you this morning?"

"I know what you said this morning."

"Well, now it's tonight and I'm sitting here having a drink. I just did ten days in jail and it doesn't make a shit to me one way or the other whether you can score for me or not. I have other sources. Okay?"

Leach turned his head, and spoke to the bar mirror. "Don't get pissed, man. I'm just always a little paranoid about dealing with new people. . . . I'm ready to deal tonight if you're ready. No shit."

"Now that you're through with the cat-and-mouse

game, go get me a sample. I'll take a look at it, and then we'll talk business."

"I'll have to take a little trip to get the stuff. After you see a sample, how long before you can have the buy money?" Leach's hand explored his face again.

"It's five minutes away," Carr said.

"Do you have any objections to showing me the money before I go make a commitment to my man? He's going to ask me if I've seen the buy money. . . . You know how it works."

The black man was intently watching Leach. He kept swishing the ice cubes in his drink, trying to look nonchalant. The blonde had moved next to Kelly.

"You'll just have to tell him that I don't show money until he shows a sample. My mother always told me that walking into traps was bad for my health."

"Okay. Okay. I'll go get a sample. I'll be back here inside of an hour. No shit. Be ready to deal in five minutes after I show the sample."

Leach got up and walked quickly out the door. The black man looked at his wristwatch.

Kelly brushed past Carr on his way to the men's room. He returned to his barstool shortly.

Carr ordered another drink and walked into the stinking men's room. He locked the door. Reaching under the sink he felt for the tape and pulled it off with the note.

Spade is a lookout, shoulder holster. I take him. Push for parking lot. Too many people inside.

Carr threw the note in the toilet, pulled the handle, and watched it disappear. He returned to his stool.

The bar phone rang. Gabe answered and stretched the cord to reach the black man. He listened, said, "Right on," and gave the phone back to Gabe.

Leach came back within a few minutes. He walked in the door and looked around nervously. The black man gave a subtle nod.

Leach walked to Carr and handed him an envelope.

"Let's go out in the parking lot. There's too many people in here," Carr said. He placed the envelope in the pocket of his sports coat and walked toward the door. Leach followed him closely, looking about. The black man put money on the bar.

Carr stepped out the front door onto Hollywood Boulevard. He took the envelope out of his pocket, opened it, and saw four twenty-dollar bills. The serial numbers were the same.

Leach was walking ahead of him now, into the parking lot. Carr saw the black man come out the rear door into the dark parking lot with his hand inside his leather coat. Where was Kelly?

Leach stopped suddenly and faced Carr. "You looked at the samples," he said. "Now lemme have 'em back and you go get your fuckin' buy money."

"Sure," said Carr. He handed the envelope to Leach.

Kelly came out the back door. It was time. Carr reached into his back pocket, removed a handkerchief, and threw it to the ground. With a puzzled look, Leach focused on the handkerchief for a moment and then looked back at Carr.

Kelly jumped the black man from behind. They fell, struggling, to the asphalt, behind a row of parked cars.

Carr pulled his .357 magnum and pointed it at Leach's face. "Federal officer! Freeze!" He pulled his coat back, showing the badge on his belt.

Leach dropped the envelope and raised his hands.

The sound of fist striking flesh and the rattle of handcuffs came from behind the parked cars. Kelly stood up, holding a .45 automatic for Carr to see. "I got him," he said, out of breath.

Kelly got in the back seat with the handcuffed prisoners for the ride to the field office.

In the interview room, Leach picked at his face as Carr filled in the arrest forms.

"Is that a two-way mirror on the wall behind you? No shit?"

Carr continued to write.

"Why don't you warn me of my constitutional rights?"

"No need to. You are bought and paid for. You delivered four counterfeit twenties to the man."

"I think I was entrapped into the whole thing. No shit. You asked me to score some paper for you in the county jail. I was just doing you a favor. . . . Why were you in my cell in the first place?" He squeezed something on his neck and looked at his fingers. He wiped the fingers on his pants.

Carr completed the last of the redundant paperwork. He put his pencil down and offered Leach a cigarette.

"Thanks. No shit." Leach pulled the cigarette from the pack and hung it from his mouth. He lit it with a flourish.

Carr spoke softly. "Pleach, you've been around. I think you and I can talk turkey. I'll be up front if you will. What *I* want is the names of everybody you've dealt the twenties to, and the location of the rest of the stash. What do *you* want?"

Leach pulled the cigarette from his mouth and looked Carr in the eye. "It doesn't matter what I want or don't want 'cause I ain't saying a fuckin' thing. And that is no shit." His expression was smug.

"You must be one of those freaks who actually *likes* the joint. Is that it?" Carr said. He leaned back in his chair.

"I like the joint about as much as I like sticking my head into a bucket of pure shit. But I've been around long enough to know that since I'm on parole I'm going to be violated. I'll pick up another eighteen months, of which I'll have to do a third. Your case with the four twenties will be dropped by the U.S. atttorney in the interest of justice so as not to clog up the court since I'm already going back to prison. After all, four twenties is only eighty bucks. With good time, I'll serve four months, and probably only three, since December is early-out time. So, for ninety days you want me to be a snitch and take a chance on getting a shiv stuck up my ass? No way. No fuckin' way. When I was a kid I once did ninety days for getting caught with one roach. I can do ninety days standing on my head."

Carr knew he was right. "If you don't want to

cooperate, I guess I'll have to go to your pad and search it. If Vikki's there with the stash, she gets arrested. Do you want to get her involved?" Carr spoke clearly.

"What the fuck do I care? She's just a dumb hype bitch. A friend of mine gave her to me. If you go there and find counterfeit money, it's hers, not mine. I didn't know what was in the envelope I gave you. Why don't you just book me? Fuck all this yakety-yak. No shit." He folded his arms across his chest.

Carr gathered up the stack of printed forms. He stood up and opened the door.

Kelly was waiting in the hallway, eating a large greasy doughnut. "Any luck?" He spoke with his mouth full.

"Nope. You?"

"The spade says he knows Pleach from the Paradise Isle. Acts as a lookout for him when he does deals. Pleach gives him a few bucks after the deal goes down. That's all he's gonna say." Kelly gulped some of the doughnut. "He's con wise, told me what I already know. He just did six months for killing his next-door neighbor; he's out on an appeal or something. Can you imagine that? Six months . . . I'd like to kill my next-door neighbor's kid. His motorcycle is too loud. Six months couldn't be all that bad." He rammed the last of the doughnut into his mouth and chewed. "I'm going down to the grand-jury room. Pick me up there when you're ready to go."

Carr walked down the hall into the tech shop and switched off the tape recorder labled "Interview Room #1." He removed the cassette tape, wrote "Arrest interview: Defendant Virgil Leach" on its label, and placed it in his shirt pocket. He looked at his watch. It was 8:00 A.M.

$/9

It was 9:30 A.M. by the time Carr had finished briefing Delgado and making phone calls to the coroner's office. He left the field office and took the elevator to the ground floor.

When the elevator door opened, he walked down the marbled hallway toward a large set of wooden doors with gold lettering that read FEDERAL GRAND JURY. A small cardboard sign hung on a door handle. DO NOT ENTER. GRAND JURY IN SESSION. On one side of the doorway stood four long-haired men, whispering to one another. They wore open-collared shirts, tight pants, gold necklaces and rings. They looked at him as if a badge was pinned to his coat.

Farther down the hallway Kelly leaned against the marbled wall.

"What's it look like?" Carr said.

"That paper-pushing sumbitch Tommy the Hat has been on the witness stand for the past hour and a half," he whispered. "He won't even give so much as his home address. The court stenographer walked out a couple of minutes ago and told me. His asshole friends are standing over there with

79

ants in their pants waiting to see if he is going to give up on them as being the ones who passed the fifties." Kelly spoke in a defeated tone. "But Tommy's being a real stand-up guy. . . . That's because he knows we don't have a good case on him."

"Why not?" Carr said.

"A bad search warrant."

"Dry hole?"

"No. We found thirty-five grand in fifties under his bed. Problem is the typist made a mistake and typed the wrong date on the search warrant."

Carr shook his head.

The grand-jury doors opened. Curly-haired and freckled, Tommy the Hat, in a French-cut white suit, was the first one out. He tapped a matching Stetson with a silver band onto his friz.

Carr walked directly up to him and grabbed his hand before he reached his friends. Tommy looked surprised.

"Tommy," Carr said, cranking the young man's hand in wedding-reception style. "The truth never hurt anybody. You've kept your part of the bargain, and Uncle Sam will keep his. Thanks again, buddy."

Tommy the Hat pulled his hand away from Carr as if it were a handcuff. The young hoods glanced at one another and turned their backs. They swaggered down the hallway without looking back. "I ain't no fucking stool pigeon!" screamed Tommy. "I didn't say a word in there." He pointed at Carr. "You . . . you . . . motherfucker!"

Carr winked at the now red-faced man and

headed down the hallway toward the exit. Walking next to him, Kelly made guttural sounds to try to keep from laughing. They passed through the revolving doors into the parking lot, and Kelly burst into hysterical, booming laughter. "How do you ever think of that shit?"

Kelly parked in front of the stucco apartment house next door to Leach's place.

Carr picked up the microphone from the glove compartment and gave the location. He replaced the microphone and shut the compartment.

"Why don't you take the rear," he said. He opened the door and got out. Kelly drove around the corner.

Carr waited for Kelly to get into position. He heard a loud whisper coming from a ground-floor window of the apartment house. "Are you a policeman? I saw you talk on the car radio." The voice was old.

Carr stopped. "Who wants to know?"

"The people in that house are up to no good," said the woman. "The girl is a doper. She passed out on the front lawn once. She lives with a guy who beats her like a dog. People go and come at all hours. I hope you arrest them."

"What's your name?"

"I don't want to get involved," she whispered.

Shaking his head, Carr walked to the front door of the house and knocked.

A tiny peephole was opened by a young woman. "Pleach isn't here," she said.

Carr held up his badge. "Open the door, Vikki."

The face disappeared from the peephole. Carr

stuck two fingers in his mouth and whistled. There was the sound of running, the back door opening, a struggle.

"Let me go!" Vikki screamed. "You're breaking my arm! You pig! Put me down!"

The screaming came toward the front door. The door was unlocked. Kelly opened the door, carrying the struggling Vikki under one arm like a calf. His other hand held a black plastic garbage bag with something in it. He handed Carr the plastic bag. It was closed with a piece of string. "She tossed this in the yard. I grabbed her before she went back in."

Carr pulled off the string and opened the bag. The money was in rubber-banded stacks. He guessed the counterfeit twenties at forty to fifty thousand worth.

Kelly sat the pale Vikki down in a bean-bag chair and began looking around the house. She was in a housecoat. Her shroud of thick dishwater hair was near waist length and caused her facial features to appear tiny. She had bony hands.

Carr sat on the couch facing a wall papered with a blown-up photo of Leach and Vikki standing in front of a Cadillac in silly poses. There was a stereo system on shelves and on another wall. The room had the scent of marijuana and dirty clothes.

Carr rested the plastic bag on his lap and read the "Warning of Rights" card out loud.

Vikki stared at the floor.

"Do you understand your rights?" he asked, putting the card back in his coat pocket.

"I've been arrested twelve times. What do you think?"

82

"Are you willing to answer a few questions for me, Vikki?"

She wrapped hair around a finger, pulled, and let it pop back. She looked at her lap. "I guess."

Carr patted the plastic bag. "Who has Pleach been peddling this to?"

"I don't know what's in the bag."

"Then why did you throw it out the back door?"

"I don't know why. I just got scared."

"Pleach is in jail," Carr said.

"For what?" She looked up.

"For delivering some of the twenties out of this bag. He was setting up a buy."

Vikki sat up straight and folded her arms across her chest. "Pleach is my old man. I ain't going to say anything to hurt him. He's been good to me."

Carr sat for a while checking the serial numbers on the counterfeit money.

A tear rolled down Vikki's cheek.

"How old are you, Vikki?" Carr asked.

"Twenty-two." Her voice cracked.

"Any children?"

Vikki turned toward him and finger-rolled some hair. "A three-year-old boy. He's with my mother because he's hyperactive. My mom didn't like my ex-old man, so she keeps him. He's really wild. It's my first husband's fault."

"What was your first husband like?"

"He used to go berserk," she said.

"How do you mean?"

"Like one time when I was out with the girls and when I came home he jumped up and threw a fishbowl at me, and it broke and all the fish were jumping around on the floor and he was grabbing my hair and hitting my head on the sink. He was bad news. He cut his hand on the fishbowl and started wiping the blood on the walls and everything."

"What happened then?"

Vikki wiped her nose with her thumb and index finger.

"I called the cops. They came and arrested him, and to get back at me he told them there was grass in the cupboard and the cops arrested me, too. I tried to make a phone call to my mom, and the cop grabbed the phone out of my hand and handcuffed my hands behind me, and I was in my housecoat and it was open in front. It was really bad news. It was really gross." She released a finger roll of hair. It sprung back to her head like a rubber band.

"When did you meet Pleach?"

"About six months ago. He was a friend of my ex-old man. The second one."

"Does Pleach score for you?"

Vikki extended her track-marked right arm. She rubbed one of the scabs as if the arm was not attached to her body.

"Yes. But I'm not saying anything else. Pleach is my old man. He told me he'd kill me if I ever snitched. Once he knocked me out. He slugged me in the jaw with all his might and knocked me out, but he didn't mean to. . . ."

"Pleach didn't stand up for you today, Vikki. Why do you think we came here?"

"I'm not going to say anything against my old man." Vikki stared at her scarred arm.

Kelly walked back into the living room and began flipping up sofa cushions.

Carr sauntered into the kitchen area and opened cupboards.

Kelly's tone was disinterested. "When's the last time you fixed?" he said.

" 'Bout twelve hours ago."

"How do you feel?"

"I don't feel good. I might have to throw up."

"You'll have plenty of time to throw up in jail tonight. It'll give you something to do." Kelly chuckled.

"You're really cold, man," Vikki whimpered.

Having checked the drawers and cupboards, Carr stepped into the bedroom. An unmade water bed in a sea of dirty clothes and shoes. He waded through the clothes and opened the window. It didn't help the smell.

The dresser drawers were overflowing with a mixture of clean and dirty clothing. Under a pile of socks he found a stack of Polaroid photos. One was of a naked Vikki spread-eagled on the slimy bed, her hype's arm outstretched. Another showed her inserting a pink rubber dildo. Her expression was passive. He put the photos back under the socks.

In the next drawer down was a well-worn address book. He pulled it out of the drawer and looked under R. No Ronnie. He read every page. No one with the first name Ronnie. He put the book in his coat pocket and walked back into the kitchen.

Vikki was sobbing uncontrollably, her hands over her face.

Kelly looked toward the kitchen and winked.

Carr went back into the living room and sat down next to Vikki. She looked up.

"Can I get you a drink of water, Vikki?"

Vikki shook her head no. She wiped her nose with her hands.

"I wouldn't expect you to answer any questions about Pleach if he had stood up for you, but he didn't. He handed you up."

"You're just trying to trick me into talking. I don't know anything. I don't like that other guy. He's a real prick." She pointed at Kelly. "Pleach has been good to me. He respects me as a person."

"He doesn't respect you as a person."

"How do *you* know?" Vikki whined.

Carr stood up and walked to the stereo-system wall unit. He took the cassette tape from his shirt pocket and popped it into the tape player. He fiddled with the dials and turned up the volume to loudspeaker quality.

"If Vikki's there with the stash, she gets arrested. Do you want to get her involved?"

"What the fuck do I care? She's just a dumb hype bitch. A friend of mine gave her to me. If you go there and find counterfeit money, it's hers, not mine."

Carr turned off the tape player and removed the cassette. He put it in his coat pocket and sat down next to Vikki again.

Her expression was the same as in the Polaroid photographs.

Kelly rambled through the bedroom, slamming drawers.

Vikki began to cry again. "I want to see my little boy."

"Who did Pleach give some of the counterfeit money to?" Carr said.

"Nobody. He was holding the stash for a printer

86

who went to the pen. He didn't want to pass the money because the Feds had the serial numbers. That's all I know. How much time am I going to get?" The bag is Pleach's. Not mine. Honest to God."

A tear rolled off the end of her nose and landed on the front of her housecoat.

"Think back, Vikki. Did he give even one or two of the twenties to anyone?" Carr's voice was soothing, soft.

"He gave a couple of them to a red-haired guy. 'Bout fifty years old, balding. He came over a few days ago. Told Pleach he needed a couple of the bills for a scam or something. I was in the kitchen, and I heard them talking."

"What kind of a scam?" Carr leaned closer.

"He didn't say, and Pleach didn't ask."

"What was the man's name?"

"Red That's what Pleach called him. That's all I know. Honest to God."

"Does Pleach know anybody named Ronnie?"

"Not that I know of." Vikki grabbed her stomach. "I think I have to throw up . . . right now." Carr followed her to the bathroom. She gagged and wretched into the sink violently.

"The mating call of the hype," Kelly said.

Carr leaned against the bathroom doorjamb.

"We might have just run out of luck," Carr said.

"What?"

"She says the only bills went to somebody named Red. That's all she knows. I believe her."

"Unless we can come up with a 'Red,' we're at the end of the road," Kelly said.

Carr nodded.

$/10

At the East L.A. County women's jail, Carr had written "Possession of Counterfeit Notes—Federal Arraignment" on Vikki's booking sheet while Kelly had squirted her vomit off the back seat of the G-car with a garden hose.

After finishing the usual booking procedures, Carr phoned Delgado and filled him in. It was 9:30 P.M.

On the way to the field office, Kelly stopped at a taco stand on Brooklyn Avenue.

They got out of the car and walked to the painted hut. GOMEZ BROS TACOS CARNITAS. A freckled face came to the window and asked for their order in Spanish. Carr and Kelly looked at one another before ordering. The taco man had red hair and was balding. Carr shook his head. It had been a week since Rico had been killed and there still were no real leads. He knew as well as any cop that the longer the investigation took the less chance there was for success. Kelly ate five tacos with extra sauce, and they headed for the field office.

Delgado was waiting in the records room, sitting at a long table covered with stacks of five-by-eight arrest cards, Styrofoam coffee cups, and dirty ashtrays.

"The guys that pulled this caper had to know about how a counterfeit deal is done," Delgado said. "I think it's best if we go through the arrest cards, starting at the most current, and work backward. I've got people at LAPD records checking for the same thing. The arrest card has the color of hair and the date of birth." Delgado picked up a stack of cards and began thumbing through them.

The cards of red-haired men began to pile up in the middle of the table as the night wore on. By 3:30 A.M. they had compiled one hundred forty-six arrest forms of persons fitting the general description. Kelly, using a clerk's push cart, pulled the one hundred forty-six arrest packages from file drawers, and the three agents dug out photographs of each man, tossing them into a pile.

"Listen to this," Kelly said. He read from an arrest card: "Identifying marks: Tattoos of devil shoveling coal on each buttock." Kelly laughed hysterically. "This freak has tattoos of the devil shoveling coal into his ass!" They roared.

An hour later Carr rubbed his eyes. "Let's catch a couple of hours," he said. Kelly's head was already down on the table.

Arriving home a half hour later, Kelly parked his car in the driveway, because the garage was filled with bicycles of various sizes. He went in the kitchen door, switched on the light, and took lunch meat and beer from the refrigerator.

Sitting at the kitchen table, he chewed slowly, as if in a trance. He was exhausted.

He looked up as his wife walked into the

kitchen buttoning her housecoat, removing her long braids from inside its collar.

"Do you want me to fix you something?"

He shook his head and took a long pull from the beer bottle, wiping his mouth with the back of his hand.

"What's new around here?" he said.

"Stevie got an F in spelling. Jimmy and Junior took their bikes apart and left them all over the garage floor. That's about it."

"Uh-huh."

She would not ask him about work. That issue had been resolved early in their marriage. He didn't like to talk about the job, because there were too many things to explain, too many impossible translations. It had been easier to sever the ties between the two worlds.

Such things had really never been a problem between them. They had never tried to change one another.

Removing a crayon and coloring book from a kitchen chair, she sat down, softly rubbing her eyes.

"Do you want to talk?"

"Yeah, uh, sure," he said with lunch meat in his mouth.

"This is the earliest you've been home since it happened."

"I guess you're right." He stopped eating momentarily and unloosened his tie.

"I went to early Mass this morning and prayed for Rico. I've had nightmares about it. I've been worried about you, too." She stared at her folded hands.

"God bless you, Rose." He patted her hands. "Everything will be back to normal pretty soon."

"How could they do that to someone? Take someone's life . . . a young man like he was. He'll never be able to have . . . raise children, to have a family."

He looked away from his wife's eyes.

"Are you going to come to bed?" Rose said.

"Can't sleep right now. I think I'll watch TV for a while." He put things back in the refrigerator.

Rose got up and went into the bedroom.

Kelly fell asleep after watching ten minutes of a Richard Widmark movie. He awoke an hour later and telephoned Carr at his apartment. No answer. He phoned Sally's place. Carr answered.

"Just thought of something," Kelly said. "There used to be a red-haired stickup man that hung around that bail-bond place on North Broadway. . . ."

"He's in San Quentin."

"You sure?"

"Yes. Delgado thought of him and had him checked out."

"Oh. Uh. Sorry to wake you up."

"Good night, Jack."

"Good night."

Carr hung up the phone on the nightstand.

"Who was that?" Sally said.

"Kelly."

"Do you feel like playing?"

"I don't know. Do you?"

She rolled away from him and mumbled something.

"What say?"

"I said *never mind.*"

Carr thought about the Sunset Motel again.

It was 8:00 A.M. Driving back toward the women's jail, Carr wondered if it would have been better not to try to sleep at all. The fatigue had set in.

"What happens if Vikki doesn't recognize any of the mug shots?" Kelly said, looking blankly at the road.

"Back to square one," Carr said. He yawned.

While putting their service revolvers in the jail safety locker, a hefty matron in a green uniform told them that Vikki had just bailed out. The lady sheriff's glossy lipstick was painted slightly over the edges of her lips, giving her mouth a gigantic appearance.

"Bail bondsman from the San Fernando Valley," she chirped. "He had an order from a judge."

"Well, I'll be god damned," Kelly said. "You might have figured that some Communist judge would screw things up."

"Communist?" the heavily rouged deputy said, smiling.

"That's right, sweet meat. Why else would a judge release a hype on bail? Hypes are sick. They couldn't find their way back to court even if they wanted to."

"Well, they all do it these days."

"That's because they're all Communists. Lawyer Communists. All judges were lawyers once. Don't forget that."

"I guess I never looked at it quite like that." The deputy adjusted a straining bra strap.

Carr and Kelly walked across the parking lot to

the government sedan. "I hope Vikki went back to Leach's place," Carr said. "Otherwise we might never be able to find her." He put the stack of mug shots in his coat pocket. He really hoped Vikki was home.

Kelly parked the sedan in the driveway of the pink apartment house next door to Leach's.

"Watch this," Carr said. He stuck his head out the passenger window and spoke in a loud whisper toward the apartment house.

"Is she home?"

"Came in two hours ago in a taxi. She's alone. Why'd you let her go?" said the woman.

"She bailed out," Carr answered. He opened the door and got out of the sedan. Kelly followed.

"Who the hell is that?" Kelly said.

"I don't know," Carr said.

They walked to the front door. Kelly knocked loudly. There was no answer. The house was still.

Kelly stayed at the front door. Carr walked along the driveway and into the back yard. He knocked on the screen door and waited. No answer. Cupping his hands to his eyes, he leaned forward against the screen. Vikki was at the corner kitchen table. Quietly, he felt the door handle. It was unlocked. He opened the door and stepped into the kitchen. Hothouse air. A burner on the gas stove was on.

Vikki was sitting in the greasy wallpapered breakfast nook, in a dinette chair. A fixing spoon, cotton ball, and an open can of dog food decorated the table. She leaned forward, resting her head on the Formica table as if taking a nap, her right arm, palm up, outstretched.

The syringe was still in her arm.

Carr touched her neck with two fingers. He could tell she was dead.

He sat down resignedly at the table, not concerned about disturbing the evidence. It was accidental, and if it wasn't, he knew there was no way to prove otherwise in an overdose.

Kelly came in the back door.

"We're back to square one," Carr said. He looked at Kelly.

Kelly turned slightly pale. He stepped back.

"O.D.?" Kelly's voice was thick.

Carr nodded.

"I'll get to the radio," Kelly said. He trotted out the back door.

Carr removed the stack of photographs from his pocket and shuffled through them.

$/11

The doors of the postwar apartments faced a cement rectangle the width of a boxing ring. On the window sills were red clay pots containing cacti and other succulents, some of which were alive. The area smelled of fried food.

Red Diamond knocked three times on a screen door that had a sign saying MANAGER.

A middle-aged woman in a helmet of hair rollers opened the door. She wore a housecoat.

He asked about Mona as if he had a right to.

"Mona Diamond?" she said. "She moved out of apartment number four about two years ago. Who wants to know?"

"Routine credit investigation," said Red. "She's applied for a loan with our company."

The woman nodded tediously, as if she had something better to do.

"Was she living with anyone?"

"Lived alone. Seldom saw her with anyone. Once in a great while some man would spend the night and leave the next morning. Different guys. This only happened every couple of months. She kept to herself. Did you know her husband was in prison? Some kind of a confidence man. Apparently he really dumped on her. She hated him."

Red shook his head calmly.

"That's all I know about her. Nice gal. Kept to herself. No parties." The woman took a bobby pin from the pocket of her housecoat and plunged it into one of the hair rollers. "Is there anything else?"

"Where did she work?"

"She was a waitress—you know, coffee shops, restaurants—nothing too fancy."

"Where is she working now?"

"I saw her a couple months ago at a coffee shop about six blocks from here. It's on Wilcox below Hollywood Boulevard . . . the left side. . . . Who did you say you were with?"

"National Credit Bureau," said Red.

"I always ask. You never know who you're talking to these days. There's millions of rapists and stranglers. I hate like hell to even open the door."

"Yes, ma'am," said Red in patrolman style. "Thanks for your help." He walked away holding his breath.

Though dark, it was still sweltering in Hollywood.

Red parked the Cadillac in front of the bay window of the Movieland Coffee Shop. He got out of the car and walked to a sidewalk pay phone without taking his eyes off Mona. Looking bored, she served steaming coffee to customers at the counter. He dropped a dime in the telephone.

A woman answered. "Sovereign Rent-a-Car, Hollywood office. This is June speaking."

Red cupped his hand around the mouthpiece.

"Hello, June. This is Dr. Richard Sanders. I rented a Cadillac from you two weeks ago."

"Dr. Sanders . . . uh . . . we've been expecting you to return the car. Your contract was a two-day rental."

"That's what I called about. I'm in Phoenix for a heart surgeons' convention and I just wanted to let you know I'll have the car back to you in another week or so."

"Oh . . . well, I guess that will be okay. It's just that you didn't have any credit cards. . . ."

"Young lady, I certainly wouldn't *call* if I didn't intend to pay for the rental."

"Certainly, doctor. I apologize if . . ."

"No problem. See you in a week."

"Thank you for calling, doctor."

Red hung up the phone. He wrote "Heart Convention Phoenix" on a card in his wallet, because he knew that details were always important. Stories *must* be kept straight.

Mona wiped the counter with a rag. Red asked himself how many women over forty could be attractive, yes, *sexually* attractive, dressed in a puff-sleeved waitress uniform? Perhaps it was the combination of the tiny waist and the full, high breasts. Her blonde hairdo was the same as years ago, when she served drinks at the Sahara in Las Vegas.

Red remembered how the high rollers all had their tongues hanging out when she swished between the crap tables with trays of drinks, and the legs of a fashion model.

Though she could have had anyone she wanted at that time, it was he who had ended up at the Chapel of Dreams saying vows, with a young

Tony Dio as best man. It was in the frenetic days of casino credit, room service, and quick, solid scores; his partner, Tony Dio, bringing in the suckers from Atlanta and Chicago to buy stock, land, and gold that didn't exist.

Mona flitted along the counter, filling cups again from a steaming glass pot. She was making her best thin-lipped smile.

Red rolled up the Caddy's windows and concentrated for a moment on relaxing, then tightening, his stomach muscles. It was his own device for trying to calm nervous intestines.

He got out of the car and walked across the street to the coffee shop. With a deep breath for sphincter control, he swung open the glass door and walked in. He took a seat at Mona's section of the counter.

Her back to him, she arranged plastic-wrapped crackers around a bowl of soup. Knowing her temper, he would not be surprised if she saw him and slammed the soup and crackers directly in his face. That's the way she was: quiet, almost docile until anger flamed. Once, in the parking lot of the Stardust Casino she almost scratched a would-be mugger's eyes out. "Cherokee Indian blood," she always said.

"Hi, Mona," he said in the softest tone he could muster.

She turned and frowned at him as if she had known he was there. She placed the soup bowl in front of a black man wearing a gas-station uniform farther down the counter. Then she picked up silverware and a napkin from a box and placed them in front of Red.

"I thought I'd just stop by, now that I'm out," he said.

Mona took a pencil and order book from her skirt pocket. "I heard you were out. May I take your order?" She leaned on one foot.

"After all this time you don't have to be so hostile," he said.

"What do you want?"

"I just thought we could talk."

"About what?" Mona snarled. She glanced around to see if anyone was listening. "One of your *big ideas* that everyone else ends up paying for?" Tomahawk eyes.

"I'll take a cup of coffee," Red said.

She served the coffee and kept busy with other customers as he drank it. His guts felt mushy. He restrained the bathroom urge.

"What time do you get off?" he said as Mona flashed by with a pie à la mode.

"Eleven," she mumbled without looking at him.

He sat for a half hour fiddling with cream, sugar, and spoon. Finally she returned.

As she made out the check for the coffee, Red spoke in his best bedside manner. "I want to talk to you about something important. It'll just take a couple minutes. Can I meet you out in front when you get off work?"

"Wait out in front," she said without looking up, and handed him the check.

Outside in the Caddy Red looked at his watch over and over again. He knew he couldn't expect wonders. After all, it had been five years. But looking at it realistically, the foot was in the door, and the first step was always the hardest. It wasn't as if he hadn't conquered her once, tamed her hot little ass and made her legs stick straight up in the air when they screwed. The facts as they stood were that she *had* agreed to meet him. He struck his hand down in his pants and adjusted his genitals.

At 11:00 he broke into a sweat. He knew once she was in the car it would be easy to talk her into joining him for a drink, and with good ol' Mona, liquor was always quicker. At 11:15 he wondered if his watch was slow.

He walked back inside the coffee shop and spoke with a young waitress. "Mona? She just got off a few minutes ago. Went home." She pointed. "Left out the back door. She always goes out that way."

Red barely made it to the men's room.

It was after 9:00 P.M. when Carr arrived at his apartment. The one-bedroom place was generally in order. It contained a sofa, TV, kitchen table and chairs, and not much else. Affordable apartments near the beach were small.

In the bedroom, he took the gun and handcuffs off his belt and laid them in a dresser drawer. The framed picture on the dresser was of his mother and father in front of the old frame house in Boyle Heights where he had grown up. The picture was the only one he had framed. The others, of him and his army buddies, police buddies, agent buddies, mugging around beer-bottled tables, were stuffed away somewhere along with the yearly pistol-marksmanship plaques.

The furniture and carpet had the musty smell that things near the beach get; and the brick-and-planks bookcase in the living room (James Jones, a few spy novels and law-of-evidence books) was visibly dusty. As Sally said, "The whole place could use a thorough and complete cleaning."

The phone rang. It was Sally.

"How about dinner along the strand somewhere?" she said. He could tell she had been drinking.

"Sure."

"Let's ride," she said.

They leaned their bikes against a front window of the restaurant. The foot-high Cyrillic-style letters on the window read PRINCE NIKOLA OF SERBIA—YUGOSLAV FOOD.

Attached to the front door was an almost life-size photo of a tall muscular man wearing wrestler's trunks and a metal-studded championship belt. He was flexing his arms and, with the exception of heavy Slavic eyebrows, was completely bald.

They went in. The tables were filled with tanned beach types. Blonde, stringy-haired young women and frizzy-haired men, all wearing garish T-shirts and sports pants.

From behind a small wine bar in the corner, Prince Nikola of Serbia, wearing a form-fitting T-shirt and white trousers, waved them to a table. He rushed over with menus and a bottle of wine. His accent was heavy. "Sarma—stuffed cabbage—is only thing left that's any good. I tell you truth, Charlie." He poured wine into two glasses.

"Sounds okay to me, Nick," Carr said.

Sally nodded agreement. She picked up the wine-glass and drank fully half of its contents.

"Did you read in the newspaper about the man

on trial for raping his wife? The judge was talking about it. A landmark prosecution." She swished her wine and sipped.

Carr nodded.

"I hope he gets convicted," she said.

"Uh-huh."

"What do you think about it?" She looked at the ceiling.

"About what?"

"About whether a man can be charged with raping his wife."

Carr looked out the window. "I guess maybe he could be charged with stealing his own car, too. Or with indecent exposure when he gets out of the shower."

Sally shook her head and pursed her lips. She filled her wineglass.

"I want to talk about us," she said.

"Go ahead." Carr hoped Nick would hurry with the food.

Sally's mouth was set straight. It was the "let off steam" look. "It just seems that things have changed between us. We don't talk any more." She sipped her wine. "Not that you *ever* were the most open person in the world. I'm not trying to start an argument." More wine. "I've talked to a lot of other women in my Wednesday-night sensitivity class who have the same problem. There's this hostility now between men and women. Both are afraid to be taken advantage of. It's not that I want to be married; I was married once. It was too restrictive for me. I just think that our relationship could become closer." Her voice cracked. She took another gulp of wine. "We've known each other for years. We just seem to be drifting.

We go to restaurants, you just sort of drop in to my apartment now and then. . . . You're too self-contained. It's almost as if you don't need other people . . . and you don't relate well to new people."

"That's just the way I am," Carr said.

"I *know* how you are. It took me years to understand you. It's because of your background. The army, the police department, then one field office after another as a Treasury agent. All the crap. Your life experiences have made you unable to show emotion."

Prince Nikola of Serbia brought another bottle of wine, winked at Carr, and poured.

"Maybe I should join your sensitivity class. I'm interested in the part where you stand around in a circle and goose the person next to you, or whatever it is they do."

"You haven't understood a word I have said," Sally said. "We are not *relating* to one another right this very minute."

It was more of the same during the meal, Sally picking at her food and drinking wine until her lips had a purplish tinge. By coffee time, she was in the "rut" phase.

"An absolute rut," she said. "You go to the same Thursday-night fights with the same friends. You even go to the same restaurants. The same bars in Chinatown. I mean, do you know how many times we've been to *this very* restaurant?" She was beginning to slur.

"Nick is a friend of mine," he said.

"That's not the damn point!" She slapped an open palm on the table.

Riding back along the dark Santa Monica

strand, Sally weaved slightly from side to side and continued to speak. She used the words *need, relate, affection,* and *dialogue* over and over again.

By the time they got to her apartment, she had begun to cry. No sobs, just the usual controlled-anger tears.

Inside, she took a bottle out of the refrigerator and poured wine. Then she sat in the middle of the living-room floor holding her wineglass with both hands.

Carr sat down next to her. He stared at the floor. "There is something serious I've been wanting to say to you for a long time. I just haven't been able to get up enough guts to say it."

Her look was incredulous. She set her wineglass down and put her hand on his shoulder. "What is it?" she said softly.

Carr leaned close to her face, his lips next to her ear. "I'm a sex fiend," he whispered. He stuck his tongue in her ear and wrapped his arms around her.

Sally tried not to giggle as she made a half-hearted attempt to struggle.

"Charlie, stop! You're making fun of me!"

He kissed her lips and reached to unzip her pants.

They made wine-prolonged love on the living-room floor. Afterward, Carr carried the nude and sleepy Sally to her bed. He pulled a cover over her, and she said "I love you" without meeting his eyes.

"I love you, too," Carr mumbled.

He dressed and bicycled back to his apartment. After showering, he wrote a note and dropped it in the drawer next to his holster and badge. It read:

1. Check mug books.
2. Ballistics report.
3. Autopsy report.

He went to bed.

$/12

The secretary ushered Red Diamond into a pan-
eled office. The little lawyer sat at a big elevated
desk with nothing on it but polish. He stuck out a
two-ringed hand and forced a smile.

"Glad to see you out," he said.

"Hi, Max."

Max Waxman's bald head was fish skin
stretched tightly over skull, with ear-level black
hair falling limply over his collar. He wore thick
glasses and a sparse mustache. His tie was white
silk. "What can I do for you?"

"Now that I'm out, just thought I'd stop by to
say hello."

"Hello." Max looked at his watch. He folded his
hands.

Red sat down lightly in the leather chair. He
nervously curled his toes inside his shoes. His
stomach was sour.

"I might as well get right to the point. I'm getting ready for a big score—an oil-lease project—
and I'm looking for backing. I thought I'd give
you first shot at it since you and me go way back.
I got the project figured for two or three hundred

grand in twenty days. I'm planning to bring the suckers in through real-estate people. The pitch is a grand a piece. I got a guy who can make the phony oil-lease charts. . . ."

"Red, *please*." The lawyer held up his hand. "I know you just got out, how tough it is and all, but these things involve too many people. The cops are on to you. You've been down too many times."

"So you won't even let me finish telling you . . ."

"I'll finish it for you. You need a front. An office, a secretary, a car, juice money for the real-estate people, the boiler room, bleepety bleepety bleep. And you want money from me. I'm sorry, Red. The answer is no. I'm sorry." He adjusted his tie.

Red sat for a moment without speaking. "Okay, then," he said, "will you loan me twenty-five grand? You know I'm good for it."

"The people that put up front money for you five years ago wouldn't think you're good for it. They went to the cleaners. They ended up sucking wind."

Red's face flushed. "And I went to the stinking, fucking joint."

"I'm sorry." Max pressed the intercom buzzer and told the secretary to make golf reservations for four, including Judge Brooks.

"If you need bucks, bring something to me, but please, nothing less than a pound. Coke should be legalized anyway. Or paper, bonds, stocks—something that's tangible. My investigator handles the arrangements. Same as before. I like to stick with the basics. Nice talking with you, Red. I'm really kind of busy today." He leaned forward and handed Red his engraved business card.

Red put it in his shirt pocket. He grasped the arms of the chair tightly. "I wouldn't ask you if I didn't need the money. I've sent you a lot of business through the years. I never handed you up to the Feds in the last project. I could of handed you up to the Feds but I didn't. They asked about you but I kept my mouth shut and walked the yard. You could have been there with me. You know that."

"I also know that the statute has run. I'm a lawyer, Red. I'm home free. They can't arrest me, because the offense happened over five years ago. That's the law. Please don't try to muscle me. Nobody muscles me. Let's remain friends." Max turned his palms up and gave a weak smile.

Red stood up and put his hands in his pockets. He thought it odd that his stomach had suddenly stopped churning.

"Tony the juice man has a long memory, doesn't he?" the lawyer asked. Red felt his head bob up and down. "I told you years ago that it was a mistake to go to him for front money. I'm sorry you didn't take my advice. I'm really very sorry."

Red walked toward the door.

"Bring something to me! Anything except grass. I have a truckload man who keeps me busy with grass. Anything else! With luck you'll be out of the bind in no time at all. I am sorry, Red." Max looked at his watch.

The door closed.

A jukebox played soul music.

Red Diamond and Ronnie Boyce sat in a corner booth with drinks, served by a floppy-breasted waitress who wore nothing but a G-string.

The only light in the bar was a semicircle of pink, which illuminated a small, round stage. On the stage, a naked blonde woman with stretch marks on her stomach arched backward clumsily to give some men at a nearby table a good look at her crotch. The men made drunken remarks of appreciation.

No one else in the place seemed to be watching her. The tables and booths buzzed with whispered negotiations of all kinds. In the next booth an older man with a ponytail and a fat Mexican woman snorted from a tiny spoon.

Red handed Ronnie the ten-dollar Sahara Casino chip. "Take a look at it, lil' brother. I just got it today. You can't tell the difference between it and a real one. It's a sample counterfeit from the guy who makes 'me. He's an inventor, a genius really."

Ronnie rubbed the chip, tried to bend it. "Can we get some more?"

"That's the problem. The inventor made up this sample for me, but we need cash before he'll go into full production. We're back in a negative-cash-flow situation at this point."

Ronnie looked puzzled.

Red wrote on the paper place mat. "Cash flow → equipment → trip to Las Vegas → $100,000." He turned the place mat around to Ronnie. "This is the way I have it mapped out. We need another score to make this thing move. The dude will make the phony chips for a flat fee and we lay 'em down in Vegas. I figure we can do four or five grand at a time. We'll take our time so the pit bosses don't catch on, then we drive back to good ol' L.A. with a hundred big ones. Fifty for you, fifty for me . . . And by the way—" Red smiled and took the chip out of Ronnie's hand—"passing phony gambling chips is a *state* crime. No Feds to worry about. Once we come back across the California border we're fucking-ass home free. You like?"

Ronnie gave a noncommittal nod. "Yeah, I guess. But how about the money on the last score? Couldn't we . . ."

Red snapped his fingers. "Damn! Let me apologize . . . I thought I had told you what we have working on that end. I've been so busy. . . . Briefly, things are great on setting up the front. I have things worked out for you and me to have offices in Century City. It looks like the best thing to go for at this point is limited partnerships for food franchises or maybe gold futures. This is what the suckers will probably go for. But I need more marketing research. We can't just jump in without *knowing* we can get the suckers. Too much risk for too little profit. You know what I mean. . . ."

Ronnie looked uncomprehending. "Yeah, sure," he said.

The near-naked waitress set fresh drinks down on the table and walked away.

"Then we're together, lil' brother?" Red said.

Ronnie, with a mouth full of ice cubes, grunted.

"That's good, that's fine," said Red. "We've got a lot of irons in the fire right now, and I want to be sure we are thinking along the same lines, you know, to avoid any fuck-ups. We have to think in terms of a long-range program. To get off the ground it's a simple matter of getting that positive cash flow. . . . That gives us a backup. There's always extras. You remember the story I told you about how I got caught short? The manager of the office building walks in and asks for the rent right when I had a sucker sitting there. I mean like the dumb fuck had his wife sitting out in the car holding his life savings. I was supposed to be selling him half ownership in a gold mine and suddenly he sees I'm behind on my rent! *No way*. It was a good lesson. The farmer and his old lady drove off with their fifteen grand, but I learned a good lesson: don't get caught short. Simple." Red gave Ronnie a pet-shop-window smile.

"Remember me telling you about the lawyer? Here's his card."

Boyce accepted the business card and looked at it curiously.

MAX WAXMAN
ATTORNEY AT LAW

SUITE 4101
SUNSET CONTINENTAL BLDG.
PHONE 721-0196

"Max Waxman is strictly a money man. You talk price with him, but the hand-to-hand will be between you and his private investigator. Max never touches anything himself; finances a couple of dope deals a week the same way. He drives a Rolls-Royce."

"What size deal should I talk about?" Ronnie put the card in his pocket.

"Tell him you have a hundred and twenty-five thousand that you're willing to sell for twelve points. Make him come up with twenty-five thousand for the buy. Don't go over that or he'll smell a rip-off. He's shrewd, real shrewd." Red took out an envelope, opened it, and showed Ronnie the two counterfeit twenties. He handed the envelope to the younger man. "Take good care of these. They're the last samples we have. The dude that gave them to me got busted last night and they got his stash."

"Two phony twenties for twenty-five grand. Sounds like a fair profit." Ronnie smiled.

"And I know you've got the balls to bring it off just like the one at the motel." Red gave his best flattery look. "Oh, that reminds me. Max will never permit a deal in a motel room. He'll push for a public place, probably a parking lot or something."

Ronnie nodded, took a bite of toast, and swallowed. "Who do I say referred me?"

"Drop Stymie's name. Stymie's been a front man for Max for years. He used to impersonate a cop, take care of the heavy stuff when Max was shaking down fag movie stars back in the old days."

"You mean Stymie the old trusty from E wing?"

"That's the one." Red finished his soda water.

"What if Waxman checks me out with him?"

"No problem. Stymie got piped last week; some Mexicans. He's in the prison infirmary with his head bashed in. He can't talk."

"So there's no way Waxman can check me out?"

"No friggin' way, baby. Old Max is shrewd, but he'll bite once he sees those samples." Red felt a slight churning in his bowels.

"With this score we should have enough, right?" Ronnie asked.

"Wha . . . Oh, yeah. One hundred percent for sure! This will give us enough to set up the counterfeit-chips caper. When that's done, we'll get our phony office, bank account, everything. I've got a guy who can draw up phony oil-field charts, whatever we need for the operation. It will be *big*. We'll have the suckers ringing our phone off the hook to put in their grand." Red took out a ball-point pen and scratched figures on the place mat. "Everything depends on cash flow. We've got to *start out* big to *make it* big. We can't get in the middle and have a cash-flow problem. That's a problem area."

Red underlined some of the figures and pointed with his pen. "See? It works out to one hundred and fifty grand for each of us, after both capers. Twenty days after we start the project. And that's minimum. Complete minimum." As Red spoke the words seemed familiar. He could switch off his mind and the words would continue. Prison chatter.

The woman on the stage bent over and grabbed her ankles. She wiggled.

"This private-eye fucker—is he gonna be heeled?" Ronnie broke a swizzle stick in half.

"Always. Waxman buys him a gun permit from a judge every year. The Red guy is telling you to be careful, very careful."

Ronnie lit a cigarette and put the match in the ashtray. "I got my permit right here." He stuck out his middle finger.

Red laughed nervously.

116

$/13

"Who gave you my name?" said Max Waxman, fiddling with his teen-ager's mustache.

"Somebody I met in T. I.," Ronnie Boyce said.

"Who is somebody?"

"Stymie."

"What does Stymie look like?"

"He looks a lot like a cop, but he ain't."

Waxman smiled. "You look a little like a cop yourself."

"Your mother looks like a cop," Boyce said.

"Okay, kid, what have you got? I'm busy today."

Boyce handed the envelope to the lawyer.

Waxman lifted the flap and blew into the envelope. Holding it open with one hand, he reached into his desk drawer and removed tweezers. He took the bills from the envelope with the tweezers and examined them carefully, both sides. He tucked them back into the envelope and handed it to Boyce.

"Quantity?

"A hundred and twenty-five grand."

Waxman wrote on a yellow pad. "I've seen better, but I can offer you ten points for the package. That's twelve thousand five hundred for you."

"Thirty points is the usual price," Boyce said.

Waxman raised his voice. "Where? Off the back of a turnip truck? I'll go fifteen points but . . ."

"Twenty points is what I want. It's what I have to get to make my end. I'll take twenty percent or I walk."

Waxman took a plastic bottle of hand lotion out of a drawer, squirted a fair amount on a palm. He rubbed his hands together until the cream disappeared.

"You're a tough little bastard, aren't you? What's your name?"

"Ronnie. Ronnie Smith," Boyce said.

"And I'm Max Doe, the brother of John. Twenty points it is. I don't have time to quibble over a few bucks. That's twenty-five grand to you. It will be in hundred-dollar bills. My man will show you the twenty-five G's first, so you have nothing to worry about. Tonight, 11:00 P.M. exactly, be at the L.A. airport. There is a phone booth in parking lot D-3. You better write that down. I suggest you get to the phone booth early to avoid any problems. At 11:00 P.M. the phone will ring and you will receive final instructions for the transaction. Be ready to deliver five minutes after you pick up the phone. If the phone doesn't ring exactly at eleven, the deal is off. It means something is wrong. Any questions?" He looked at the palms of his hands.

"Who will do the deal at the airport?" Boyce said.

Waxman took off his glasses and wiped them with a handkerchief.

"One person it's not going to be is me, young man. I'm an attorney at law. You saw the sign on the door. . . . It's been nice talking with you. Come see me anytime you have something."

They shook hands.

Boyce walked through the outer office. A fat man with a full-head black toupee and cardigan sweater made a show of handing something to the receptionist. He stared at Boyce. The screen test, thought Boyce.

Ronnie parked the car next to the airport gas station. Carol looked pale; her lips were colorless.

"You just wait here until I signal you for the case," Ronnie said.

"Then what?" Carol said. She looked at the attaché case sitting between them.

"Then you bring it to me in the parking lot, hand it to me, and go straight back to the motel."

She looked at her watch. "It's ten now. When are you going to want it?"

"A little after eleven. Right now I want you to go across the street and rent another car." He pointed.

"What for?"

"Because this car is registered to *you*. That's why. After I take this guy off, somebody might grab the license plate. Rent a big car and drive it back here. Do you have a phony license that you haven't used for anything yet?"

"Yes."

"Use it." He looked at his watch. "Make it quick. The guy is going to call me at the phone booth in that parking lot at eleven." He pointed to the parking lot behind the gas station.

119

Carol was silent for a moment. A jumbo jet roared to a landing on the runway across the street.

"You're going to ice him, aren't you?" she said. Her eyes were wide.

After a moment Ronnie spoke with a sneer. "When I tell you to do something, you'd best fucking do it without a lot of chickenshit questions. After I take this dude's money tonight, Red and I are going to have enough to set up a front. We're going to parley the score today into two or three hundred grand. No more chickenshit two- and three-grand capers that cost two or three years. Do you understand?"

She nodded, her head down. He continued.

"All you have to do is rent me a goddamn car and carry an attaché case a hundred feet. Is that too goddamn fucking much to ask?"

She turned to him. "But if everything comes apart, I'll be an accessory. That's life. I've already got a ten-year parole. I don't want to go back. Ronnie, I couldn't take anoth . . ."

Ronnie grabbed her ear lobe and jerked her toward him. His voice was a violent whisper. "Don't give me that *shit* about not wanting to go back. *Nobody* wants to go back. The difference is when you say you are *never* going back. That's the difference. To do that you gotta score big, woman. Your fifty-dollar checks ain't going to keep you out. They'll put you right back in with the bull daggers. Course, I heard you didn't mind it too much this last time. A tongue wash now and then made the time go faster, right?" He shoved her head away from him violently.

She looked at him with no expression, checked

her purse for the phony license, and got out of the car. He watched her walk across the street and enter the rent-a-car office.

Fifteen minutes later she drove into the gas station in a new Ford. She handed him the keys, and they exchanged cars.

Carol watched him drive through a toll gate into the parking lot. It was nearly full. The attaché case was next to her on the seat. He wouldn't say what was in it, but she assumed it was a piece, since they had picked it up from a bus-depot locker. She undid the latches and opened. Sawed-off shotgun. She closed the lid and snapped the latches. Ronnie was nuts. He always had been. She wondered how he had found out about what had gone on in Corona. Was it because her hair was too short? Maybe he was just guessing.

Ronnie's hands were wet on the steering wheel when he stopped next to the phone booth. He turned off the ignition. He tried to think of last-minute details, because he knew that was what he should be thinking about. What if someone tried to use the pay phone?

He got out of the car and locked all the doors. A breeze of jet fuel. His hands trembled. He stepped into the pay booth and checked his watch. It was ten-fifty-eight. A few seconds later the phone rang. Waxman's secretary's voice. She was reading from something. "The man in the sweater is our representative. He is in a black Oldsmobile. Follow his instructions." The phone clicked.

A car door of a black Olds slammed two parking rows away. In the darkness the fat man came toward him in a wrestler's walk. The pompadour wig could have been a hat.

The fat man stopped and looked around the parking lot. "Are you together*" he asked.

"Who the fuck are you?"

"I work for Max. I'm here to do business." The fat man's eyes were riveted to Boyce's hands.

"You should have said so," Boyce said. "I'm together. Where's your buy money?"

The man stepped closer. "Max doesn't buy anything without seeing the full package. That's the way it has to work. It's safer for everybody. You understand." The fat man's voice had a flat, disinterested tone, like a cop giving a ticket. He folded his arms across his chest.

Boyce maintained eye contact. "I don't want to get ripped off any more than you do. When I talked with Max, he said I could show you the paper at the same time you show me the buy money. What's wrong with that? Otherwise we stand here jerking each other off about who's going to show first. Right?"

The fat man glanced around the lot. He focused back on Boyce's hands. "If I was to agree to showing at the same time, then you shouldn't have any objection to letting me search you beforehand."

Boyce spread his arms out wide, palms upturned. "Search away! I don't have a piece. You got nothing to worry about from me. The paper is nearby. All I have to do is give the come-ahead."

The fat man glanced around the lot again. He patted Boyce's torso.

Boyce cased the lot. The fat man was alone. No backup near.

"Okay," the fat man said, "you don't have a gun. Now you just stand there where I can see you and give your mule the come-ahead." He pulled up his sweater. Underneath was a canvas money belt and a .45 in a waist holder. "The twenty-five grand is in here." He unzipped the belt and flicked the edges of four stacks of hundred-dollar bills. "Now you signal your mule. If anything goes wrong, I'll kill you first." His hand was on the .45.

"Take it easy, man." Boyce's voice cracked.

He waved his hands over his head. Carol approached with the attaché case. As she came closer he felt sweat running down the middle of his back.

She handed him the case without a word and disappeared quickly into the darkness. Another jet screamed onto the runway.

"Now open the trunk of your car," the fat man commanded. "Lay the case down in it and show me the funny money. I want to count it. While you're doing that I will let you count the money in the belt. If anybody walks by, it'll look like we're just unloading the trunk or something."

"Fair enough," Boyce said. He opened the trunk with the key. The fat man stepped closer. Boyce smelled tobacco on his breath. Boyce laid the case gently in the trunk and flicked open one latch. "Let's see the money in the belt," he said.

The fat man pulled up his sweater. Boyce flicked open the other latch on the case. The man was looking down at the money belt, trying to take it off.

Boyce slammed his fist into the fat man's jaw, knocking him backward and down. Opening the attaché case with flying fingers, he grabbed the shotgun and pointed it down at the angry fat face. The barrel was in the other man's hands. He gave an animal groan.

Boyce pulled the trigger. Recoil knocked him backward into the trunk. The fat man scrambled on the ground. Boyce fired again. The fire flash spun the man's body over.

Ears buzzing, Boyce dropped the shotgun into the trunk, jumped up, and slammed the lid. He ran to the car door. The money belt! He was on the ground tearing at the sweater and the money belt. *Everything is red! Can't get it off!* The fat man gurgled. He ripped the belt from the body and ran for the car door. He jumped in, threw the car in reverse, and backed out. He felt the car running over the body, back wheels, then front wheels.

Keeping an eye on the speedometer, he drove to see Red. At a stoplight, he stuffed the bloody money belt under the seat. His hands felt sticky.

$/14

Red Diamond was waiting on the bus bench at Sunset and Gower. He was where he had said he would be.

Ronnie sounded the horn, and Red got in.

"Any problems?" Red said. He closed the car door.

"I wasted the private eye," Ronnie said. He pulled back into the Hollywood traffic.

"Where's the money?"

"Under the seat."

Red reached under the car seat. "Drive into that supermarket lot up the street on the right." He pulled out the money belt with two fingers. "Jeez."

He unzipped the belt and pulled out a stack of hundreds and began counting. "Oh, no! Oh, shit! It's a fucking gypsy bankroll! The hundreds are counterfeit!"

Ronnie slammed on the brakes in front of the supermarket.

"Let's see!"

Red held out the bills. "Look! Look! We've been fucked! That rotten fucking Waxman was

125

going to trade twenty-five grand in funny money for a hundred and twenty-five grand! Paper for paper! That dirty kike!" Red slammed his fist against the dashboard.

Ronnie had a headache. His ears rang from the sound of the shotgun.

"Maybe you should have gone with me, Red."

"Uh . . . bad idea. Everybody in town knows Red Diamond—they could have followed up on us. You know. Don't worry about what happened. It's just one of those things. You know."

Ronnie shook his head from side to side.

People walked in and out of the bright supermarket. They were talkative. The heat of the day was over.

"Shit, shit, shit, " Red said, holding the bridge of his nose with two fingers.

"What are we gonna do now?" Ronnie said.

"We can recover from this if we just use our heads. This is a setback. Gotta come back. Gotta come back fast. That's the problem," Red said. His voice became rhythmic, constant, uncontrollable. He had started one of his lectures. "We can do it," he said. "Never doubt that for a minute! See the turkeys walking out of the store with their bags of potato chips? Every one of 'em has a game . . . a scam." Red pointed to a bald man in a jogging outfit carrying a carton of soft drinks in each hand. "Ten to one he's some kinda businessman. Probably like insurance. I can usually guess. . . . He's got *his* scam. That's what insurance is. They bet you will die, you bet you will live, and they always win. Insurance companies are more crooked and powerful than the whole goddamn Mafia. . . . Go down the street to the Fairfax

Towers Hotel and you can see Brother Roper's church bus load up every morning with suckers. All old people with canes. They crawl into the bus at 8:00 A.M., and Brother Roper drives 'em out to the City of Moses, a plot of land off the freeway between here and Las Vegas. There's nothing there but desert. All they have to do is sign over all their money to him and he guarantees them a home in the City of Moses as soon as it's built. He's had the same scam for ten years and never been busted! The bastard had to be a millionaire by now. . . . It's just luck. . . . You and me pull one chickenshit caper and end up with a gypsy bankroll! But we can't let it get us down. We have to be *positive.*"

Ronnie Boyce's ears buzzed.

Carol, in shorts and a halter top, bought a morning newspaper from the sidewalk rack and walked back into the hotel room reading.

"Ronnie, listen to this!" She folded the paper to the second page and read aloud. " 'The body of an unidentified man was discovered in a parking lot at Los Angeles International Airport last night. Police sources said the man had been murdered by a shotgun, in a gangland style, possibly as the result of an underworld dispute. A witness told investigators she saw two men talking at the trunk of a car and one brandished a weapon and fired twice. The police investigation is continuing.'"

"Lemme see." Ronnie, in shorts, got off the bed and grabbed the newspaper from her hands. He read, moving his lips, and threw the paper back to Carol. "They don't have anything," he said.

"Don't *have* anything? If they've got a witness, they've got somebody who can *identify* you. Pick you out of a *line-up!* Oh, God, I knew something like this would happen." She crumpled the paper.

Ronnie sat down on the bed. He leaned back against the headboard. "That's always been your problem, Carol."

"What?"

"Your problem is that you lose your cool. You get excited and you lose your cool."

Carol shook her head. "I just don't want to go back to . . ."

". . . to the joint," he interrupted. "Well, you won't have to as long as you keep your shit from getting disturbed. I used to be the same way. Everything was a big deal. But not any more. The only way to keep out of the joint is to relax, take each day as it comes. If a case comes down, you keep your mouth shut and ride the beef. Nine out of ten times if you keep your mouth shut, you can beat the case in court. That's a statistic, an actual statistic." He adjusted a pillow behind his head.

Carol spoke. "I don't want you to think I'm . . ."

"I don't think anything, Carol. I'm just telling you that I used to be dumb. That's right, dumb. Would you believe, the first time I did a bank job I didn't know that banks had robbery cameras? That's being dumb. But I'm not dumb any more. The guy I snuffed last night ain't going to take the witness stand too soon. And he was the only other person that saw what happened. Do you see what the fuck I mean?"

She sat down on the edge of the bed resignedly. "Yeah, I guess."

"It's all evidence. What the D.A. wants is evidence. Without it they can't do diddly shit. It's simple, really."

"How much money did the guy have last night?" Carol said.

"Twenty-five G's in funny money," said Ronnie. "But it's going to set up a front. My partner is a con man. He's the best. Within a month I'm going to be set for life, with no way of getting nailed. Phony land deal. There's only so many dudes that have enough smarts to pull one off. The paperwork is set up so that there's no way of getting convicted even if you stand trial. They can't prove intent."

"Sounds beautiful." Carol got off the bed and stood staring out the window.

"It *is* beautiful. We just needed some front money. I did a guy the same way for ten grand a week ago. No witnesses there either." He scratched under his arm. "Let's go get some breakfast." He went into the bathroom and closed the door. The shower started.

Carol turned on the radio fairly loud and dialed a long distance number. She stared at the bathroom door.

"Naomi?"

"Yes"

"It's Carol."

"Carol, honey, I knew you'd call. I knew you'd change your mind."

"I gotta get out of L.A.," Carol whispered. "I'm with a guy that's bad news. I'll be there this weekend. I'm gonna lay down all my paper—I've got a stack of cashier's checks—then I'm coming to you. I can't take it here any more. I'm paranoid. Can't talk now." She cupped her hand around the receiver.

"Little sister, when you get here the first thing I'm going to do is turn you inside out. I've missed you so much." A kissing sound.

Carol put down the receiver.

The shower went off.

Ronnie walked back in the room soaking wet. "What's the weird look on your face for?"

"Nothing." She gulped.

"Get a towel." He stood with his hands on his hips.

Without a sound, she picked up a towel from the dresser and began drying him. His back, chest, buttocks, legs, and groin.

"That's the way the screws choke you out in T. I."

"What?"

"With a towel." He snatched the towel from her hands, spun her around, pulled it tightly around her neck. She gagged. He flipped the towel back to her.

"Like that," Ronnie said.

Carol coughed and rubbed her Adam's apple.

"Get your clothes off, woman."

Carol stripped as fast as she could.

Without air conditioning, the field office would have been intolerable. Gray desert air hung outside. Exhaust City.

Carr got up from the desk and stared out the window at the brownstone Hall of Justice. The ninth floor was a jail and had iron windows. Five years ago a prisoner had escaped from the jail by using a homemade rope. If he remembered correctly, the man was caught the same day at his mother's house in Glendale, where he had grown up. Stupid.

"Are you sure Vikki wasn't murdered?" Delgado said. He leaned against a bulletin board with blown-up photographs of counterfeit twenties.

"We talked to the taxi driver who picked her up at the woman's jail," Carr said. "He took her straight to Leach's pad. Nonstop. A nosy neighbor saw her go into the house. Coroner set the time of death to within a half hour of when she got home. Everything points toward a simple overdose." He loosened his tie.

"I thought you and Kelly searched the pad when you arrested her. Where'd she get the dope?"

"We missed it when we searched. Inside the door handle on the service porch. It was probably an emergency stash," Carr said.

The phone rang.

"Carr."

"This is Kelly. I'm down here at the morgue. I just talked with the coroner himself. He says it was heroin, not poison or anything, and it was usual strength. She O.D.'d. See you in an hour. I gotta stop for a bite."

"Thanks." Carr put down the phone. "The coroner says she O.D.'d on smack. She wasn't murdered—unless somebody gave her a hotshot on purpose."

"I wonder if she committed suicide," Delgado said.

Carr wasn't listening. He faced Delgado. "Let's look at the big picture right now. We're looking for two suspects: a young guy and a middle-aged, balding, red-haired man. The only witness who can identify the red-haired man just checked out of the world. Leach, the man with the samples, won't talk. We've got a stack of one hundred and forty-six photos of red-haired men. That's what we've got. Nothing more, nothing less."

"Only one way to go," Delgado said.

"One way. We'll check up on every red-haired man. See what he's up to, who he hangs with. One of them has got to fit into the picture." Carr turned to look out the window.

"It's a long shot," Delgado mumbled.

"I know it."

$/15

Carr walked toward a run-down stucco house. A FOR SALE sign was stuck in the middle of the tiny yellow lawn. It was as hot as August can be, and his suit and tie felt like a damp strait jacket.

Of course, without the tie, people would never open the door. It was more important than a badge and credentials. Kelly had proved it on a Chinatown bet once by pasting a picture of a monkey over his credentials photo and conducting a whole day of interviews. No one had noticed. And as he told it at Ling's, one lady had mistaken him for an FBI agent.

Carr rang the doorbell. Immediately footsteps clacked on what sounded like a hardwood floor.

The door was opened by a tanned, middle-aged woman in a bikini bathing suit and wooden sandals. She held a *TV Guide*. Behind her he noticed Danish modern furniture, but no carpeting.

Carr flashed his badge. "Special Agent Carr, U.S. Treasury Department. May I come in?"

"Cute little badge," the woman said. "Come in." She waited for him to enter and closed the door. "What have I done to deserve a visit from a T-man?" She walked daintily to a portable bar, picked up a beer glass, and sipped.

"I'm conducting an investigation on someone who lives here in the neighborhood. I have a photo I'd like you to look at." He removed the photo from his shirt pocket. She sauntered to him and examined the photo, holding it gingerly by one corner. She blushed and handed it back.

"Which one of the nosy neighbors told you to come here?" She spoke with her teeth together.

"I may or may not have talked to your neighbors. Right now I'm talking to you. Do you know this man?" Carr took out a handkerchief and wiped his brow.

"Of course I know him; he lives next door," she said.

"Who lives with him?"

"He has a wife and three children. Is that what you mean? What kind of investigation is this?" she snarled.

"A background investigation," Carr said. "Do you know any of his friends?"

"Maybe."

Carr took out his pen. "How about some names?" he said.

She slammed her glass down on the bar and began shouting. "What do you mean 'How about some names?' Let me tell you something. This may be a low-rent neighborhood but I've only lived here since my divorce. I used to live in San Marino, but I ended up with nothing except some goddamn furniture!"

"Hold it a minute . . ." He raised his hand like a traffic cop. "All I want to know is . . ."

"No! I know one of the goddamn nosy neighbors told you to come here because he and I . . . are friends. His stupid wife started the rumors about us. Did you see the 'For Sale' sign when you walked in? That's why I'm moving."

"Lady, I'm not interested!" The woman looked foolish standing there screaming in her bikini.

"Does this have something to do with his child support? Did his first wife send you here? Can't you people give somebody a break? You've got him in jail on a failure-to-provide warrant. What else do you want—blood?"

"When was he arrested?"

"Two weeks ago. He's been in jail since then."

"Thanks. I don't have any more questions." Carr almost trotted to the door.

"Why don't you do something about dope pushers instead of nosing into people's private lives!" she shouted.

Carr walked to the car, drove around the corner, and parked. He wrote "In jail past two weeks" on reverse side of the photograph and threw it in the glove compartment with the others that had turned out to be dead-end leads.

His notations on the photos showed that three of the men were currently serving time in prison, and one was in the hospital the day Rico was murdered. Another carrot-top had been dead for over a year.

It had taken Carr all day to find these things out.

By 10:00 P.M. he had eliminated two more redheads. He drove to Chinatown and found Kelly in a booth at Ling's. The bar was full of detectives, because it was federal payday. The atmosphere was rowdy.

135

"Get this," Kelly said, digging his hand deeply into the bar peanuts. "I showed one of the photos to this guy today and he tells me he thinks the photo looks like *me*. I look at it and by God he's right! Except for the red hair, the picture did sort of look like me. I hadn't looked at it that close before. I felt like a real donkey. He must have thought I was walking around showing mug shots of myself. Do you believe that?" Throwing his head back, he accepted the entire handful of peanuts into his mouth.

Carr almost guzzled his first drink. He had been thinking about it for hours.

Rose stood at the end of the bar under a pink light, lifting drinks onto her tray. Her long black hair contrasted oddly with the bright-blue sheen of her dragon-embroidered cheongsam. Even in high heels, she was tiny, the spread of her buttocks from a tiny waist being her only striking physical quality. In the pink light of the bar, just as up close, she appeared drawn, tired, and less than happy, as if it had taken longer than usual to become forty years old.

She smiled at Carr, and gave a quick wave. He thought of how he waved at her as he drove away from her house after they had made love the first time. Standing at the window in her kimono she had waved back. He hadn't really wanted to leave. "Very embarrass when children wake up in morning," she had said, with her head slightly bowed.

He wasn't sure why he continued to see her. The meetings were infrequent and always seemed a little strained. They never had a great deal to say to one another. Her husband was dead, and she had to work, and he was a federal cop and lived at the beach. That was about it.

But he kept going back to her wan smile and the way she modestly covered her smallish breasts when she crawled into bed.

She made her way to the booth and handed Carr a Scotch-and-water. Kelly excused himself and got up.

"Sit down for a minute," Carr pointed to the seat.

She shook her head. "Too busy right now. Ling get mad."

"How was Lake Arrowhead?"

"We have a real nice time," she said. Her voice was just loud enough to be heard. "Boys catch fish in the lake. Too bad you couldn't come up one day. You probably busy. . . ."

"Yes. Uh, I . . ."

She saw Kelly coming back to the table.

"You come over tonight maybe?" She looked around to see if anyone was listening.

"Yeah. Okay," Carr said.

She shuffled back to the bar.

The bar phone rang and Ling picked it up.

"Charlie, for you." He held up the receiver.

Carr walked to the end of the bar and squeezed in between two bearded federal narcotics agents.

"Carr here."

"Higgins, LAPD Homicide. I got something for ya. Better roll down to the airport. Parking lot D-3."

"What is it?"

"Last week, in Chinatown, you asked me to let

137

you know about any capers with sawed-offs. Somebody just got blown away down here. Looks like a rip-off."

On the way to the airport Kelly remarked that they had forgotten to pay for their drinks.

Carr nodded at a uniformed policeman and ducked under the rope barrier.

A police portable light illuminated a good portion of the parking lot as well as the heavy body, face down on a blanket of dried blood. Flashbulbs snapped. People stood around wearing uniforms of one kind or another.

Higgins, in baggy pants and a short-sleeved white shirt, which concealed the shoulders of a well digger, appeared formidable in the bright light. He stood next to the body making notes on a clipboard. His belt was an array of holsters and pouches.

He nodded at the Treasury men, tucked the clipboard under his arm, and knelt by the body. He pointed with a pencil.

"See the exit wounds? Definitely a shotgun. There's no way to know for sure whether it was a sawed-off, but that's my bet. Japanese tourist lady on the other side of the lot says she saw a man shoot a . . ."—he glanced at the clipboard—" 'long fat pistol.' From what she says, he shot once, cranked another round, and finished him off, got in his car, and split. She can't give any description. Says it was too dark . . . Looky here." He pointed to the small of the back. "Fresh knife cut right here. Doesn't make any sense unless maybe he was wearing his buy money."

"A money belt?" Carr asked.

138

Higgins stood up. "That's a roger. The wound could be from getting a money belt cut off."

"Who is he?" Carr furrowed his brow.

"His wallet says his name is Michael Sawtelle and he works as a private dick for an attorney named Max Waxman. I called Intelligence just now. They have Sawtelle listed as 'Fat Mike,' a transaction man. His M.O. is to show up at a dope deal as a front man. He has his buy money tied around his waist. He shows his .45 for security, then deals right on the spot. I guess he wasn't short on balls. The deals are supposedly set up by Waxman. He's listed in the files as a money man."

"Wheels?" Kelly asked.

Higgins pointed with the clipboard. "The black Olds over there. It's clean. Registered to a car-leasing outfit in Studio City that doesn't give out info on who leases their cars. It's a caper car, for sure. Fat Mike had the car keys in his pocket."

Carr shook his head. "Doesn't look like you have too much to go on," he said.

"You're right there. I'll interview Waxman in the morning and he'll tell me he didn't know what Fat Mike was up to. I'll leave the case open for a couple of months to see if anybody will drop a dime. If nothing happens, I'll close it unsolved. Sorry, there's nothing much here to help you guys. Although it definitely could be the same guy who did Rico." He raised his voice as a plane flew over.

"It is the same guy," Carr said. He watched a policeman slide thin boards under the body. "The word is that Waxman finances counterfeit-money deals all the time. We've never been able to prove it."

A young detective in a hound's-tooth coat and styled hair motioned to Higgins from behind the rope barrier. Higgins went over to him. Four policemen grunted, hoisting the body onto a wheeled cart.

"Let's go," Carr said to Kelly. They walked to the rope and ducked under.

Higgins stopped talking to the young detective and turned toward them. "Here's one! The Japanese lady is catching the next flight back to Japan. Says she's seen enough of this country in two hours. Can you beat that?"

"See ya," Carr said.

Being careful not to make unnecessary noise, Carr unlocked the back door of Rose's tract house and sneaked down the dark hallway. He passed the door to her son's room. It was closed.

He tiptoed into a dark, air conditioned bedroom and sat down on the edge of the bed. He took off his clothes.

"I was waiting for you," Rose whispered. She crawled across the bed and began massaging his neck with miniature hands. Her nipples brushed softly against his back.

Before they made love, Rose stuffed a pillow between the headboard and the wall, as she always did to avoid waking up the children.

It was light. He groped out for his watch. Six. Rose's head rested on his shoulder. She was awake.

"I've got to get going," he said, trying to bring himself into full consciousness. He eased her head off his shoulder and got out of bed.

Dressing in front of a wall mirror, he noticed the middle-aged flesh around his waist. The children in the other room could have been his if he had married. . . .

Rose lay on her back, her eyes open, arms flat at her sides. "Ling says you maybe get a transfer," she said as he buttoned his shirt.

He turned to the dresser and picked up his holster. He clipped it on his belt and put the revolver in. "Maybe," he said, throwing on his coat.

He walked to the door.

"You come to Ling's tonight?" she said, still staring at the ceiling. Her voice was barely audible, childlike.

"Probably."

"I see you there," she said.

Carr looked down the hallway and out the back door.

$/16

It was 7:00 A.M.

The underground parking lot was cool and drafty. Carr told Kelly to pull in next to a parked delivery van. He did, and turned off the motor. Carr focused the rearview mirror on a sign, RE-SERVED—MAX WAXMAN, on the wall at the other end of the parking lot.

"Why don't we just talk to him in his office?" Kelly said.

Carr shook his head no. "His office is probably wired for sound. I've never seen an attorney that wasn't big on tape recording."

"I hadn't thought about that," Kelly said.

A half hour went by before they spoke again. The car radio buzzed with a freeway surveillance.

"You know why people become counterfeiters?" Kelly said. He was slumped down in the driver's seat, his eyes closed.

"Why?"

"Because they think it's a crime that really isn't a crime. They figure if they can make a counterfeit twenty that's good enough, they can pass it and it will go all the way to the bank. No one's the wiser.

What's a few bucks to Uncle Sam? Nobody gets hurt. That's what they figure."

Carr nodded sleepily.

Kelly continued. "Sort of like doctors who give unnecessary operations."

Waxman pulled into his parking place at 9:00 A.M. exactly.

Carr waited until Waxman took his briefcase out of the trunk and began to walk toward the elevator before approaching him.

"Mr. Waxman?"

"Yes." The lawyer looked puzzled.

Carr showed his badge. "I just wanted to ask you a couple of questions. It's about the murder of your investigator."

Waxman's tone was condescending. "I've already talked to the police. I have no knowledge of Michael's personal affairs."

"Would you mind joining me in the car for a moment so we can speak privately," Carr said.

"Can't we go to my office?" A deprecating smile.

"I'd rather not," said Carr. "I'll be happy to explain why if you'll just let me have a few minutes of your time."

Kelly pulled up in the sedan and swung open the rear door.

"I don't really understand all the secrecy, but . . . oh, what the hell." Hugging his briefcase, Waxman crawled across the back seat. Carr slid in next to him.

"This *does* seem a little overdone," Waxman said.

Kelly drove up cement ramps to the busy street.

"Stuffy down there," he said. "I'll just drive around a little bit."

"What do you people have to do with this thing? I was interviewed last night by the Robbery-Homicide people, and I'll tell you exactly what I told them. I have no control over what my employees do on their own time." He spoke carefully.

Kelly looked at Carr in the rearview mirror.

Carr spoke. "A week ago a Treasury agent was murdered with a sawed-off shotgun when he was working undercover. Someone named Ronnie and a red-haired man about fifty years old were the ones who did it. I think they were the ones who dumped your stooge last night."

Waxman leaned back in the seat with no expression. He cleared his throat. "So?"

"So I want you to tell me who they are." Carr paused. "I'll give you my word that what you say will go no further."

Waxman gazed out the window as if sightseeing. "Gentlemen, you don't really expect me to sit here in the back seat of this car and give you a statement about something I know nothing about, and thus incriminate myself, do you? In case you didn't know, I *am* an attorney at law." He turned to Carr. "Would you like one of my cards?"

Kelly stopped for a light.

"Your card says you're a money man and that you never dirty your hands," Carr said. "My partner and I respect you for that. It may sound funny, but we actually do. We know that if *you* didn't act as a middleman somebody else would. To you it's strictly a business proposition, a way to pick up a few bucks. The people who own Standard Oil and AT & T would do the same thing if they weren't making so much money in other ways. All we're asking is that you do something that is in your best interest. Last night your right-hand man got his guts blown out in a parking lot. It could just as easily have been you. The rip-off artist could have dumped you right in your office. Blown your brains out the window onto Wilshire Boulevard . . ."

Waxman frowned. "You needn't be so graphic."

"I'm not finished," Carr said.

"Excuse me."

"They probably showed you a sample; you made the arrangements and agreed on the price. They met your man and ripped him off. You have nothing to lose by helping us, by telling us what you know," Carr said.

"On the other hand, counselor, I have nothing to gain," Waxman said, smirking.

Carr waited a few minutes before speaking. "Yes, you do."

"What's that?"

"You will have our word that we will not put you completely out of business."

Waxman took out a monogrammed handkerchief and wiped his head, neck, and mouth.

Kelly accelerated onto the freeway at Ninth Street.

"Who are you people? Where are we going? What do you mean put me out of business? Jesus Christ!" Waxman said. He rolled his window down a few inches.

"I'll tell you what I mean," Carr said, leaning back in the seat. "If you don't tell us, the heat will be on full blast the minute you get out of this car. Tomorrow you and your secretary get subpoenas to the federal grand jury. I guarantee TV cameras will be there when you appear. I'll contact every one of your clients and ask them the same questions I asked you. I'll put the word out on the street that you are a snitch; that you're ready to turn on all the big dealers in town. We'll camp out in front of your office and your home. I'll dedicate my life to fucking you over. No one in his right mind would want you to back a deal. You'll be back to chasing ambulances."

Waxman grabbed the front seat with both hands. He spoke to Kelly.

"Stop the car! I want out. Let me out right this minute! Right now! I said *right now!*" He tapped Kelly's shoulder.

Kelly speeded up. "Keep your hands off me, you dirty, shit-eating bastard. You filthy, rotten, mother-fucking Communist shyster," he snarled.

Waxman's eyes became big.

Carr twisted in the back seat and faced him.

"Your crummy little brain has figured everything out, hasn't it?" Carr said. "You are going to pull every political string in town the moment you can get to a phone. You're going to call the United States attorney and every political hack in town and tell them how the T-men threatened you. You think you can get us reprimanded and taken off the case. Well, if your connections are as good as everybody says, you're probably right. We *would* be taken off the case. Nothing else would happen to us though, because you have no evidence. If we'd talked in your office, you could have recorded everything, but as it stands now, it's your word against ours, and I guarantee that we will have our story together."

The lawyer folded his arms and sat back. "I want to go back to my office. Right now. I demand to go back right now. I *insist* that . . ."

"But here's the punch line," Carr said. "After you get us taken off the case, we're going to wait until everything is just right and then we're going to catch you alone and beat you to death."

Waxman's jaw dropped. "What?"

"Beat you to death," Carr said. "We're going to beat you to death with our bare hands because we will be so pissed off. You have so many enemies in town no one will even suspect us."

Waxman turned his head. "You are threatening me," he said to the window.

"That's right, you subhuman, chickenshit pimp," Kelly said. He took the Alvarado Street off-ramp. A few blocks farther he slowed down and stopped next to Echo Park Lake. He turned off the engine. Smog-colored ducks coasted on green-ish water. The lake was outlined by graffiti-covered palm trees and overflowing trash cans.

Kelly parked and leaned an arm on the back of his seat. "I say why put off till tomorrow what you can do today?" He smiled strangely at the lawyer.

They lawyer swallowed and turned his head. He stared out the window. He cleared his throat three times. "You people are up tight for nothing. You're off base. I don't know anything that can help you. You may not believe me, but I actually have no information on the topic you are interested in. I swear to God. You're wasting your time talking to me . . . and your threats don't frighten

148

me. You want this guy pretty bad, don't you?" The lawyer's lower lip trembled. He quickly rubbed it with the back of his hand.

"All I want is what you know," Carr said. "No more, no less."

"Once I had a client who was charged with stealing some of those ducks over there; he was charged with grand-theft duck, believe it or not," said Waxman, with a nervous laugh. "He never did say what he was going to do with them. He wouldn't cop out even to me." He paused. "What makes you think a red-haired guy was involved?"

"You first," Carr said.

Waxman spoke in a monotone. "There is a chap named Red Diamond, just out of T. I., a con man, who is hurting for bucks. The sharks are after him. He came to see me a few days ago and wanted money. I shined him on. He's the only red-haired guy I can think of. Ronnie was a walk-in. He came in yesterday. I'd never seen him before. I never would have guessed Red Diamond. Red lives in Hollywood somewhere. That's all I know."

Carr nodded to Kelly in the rearview mirror.

Kelly started the engine and drove in the direction of Waxman's office. During the trip, Waxman told them three times that threats of any kind had no effect on him. Neither Carr nor Kelly spoke. Kelly pulled up in front of the modern glass structure, and Waxman got out without saying a word.

Kelly drove two blocks to a coffee shop. The waitress smiled when he asked for extra hash browns, and an extra bottle of ketchup.

"Do you think he will cause a stink?"

"I don't think so. But that's the chance you take. It's a possibility."

"Jesus, I hope not," Kelly said. "Why do you think he talked?"

"I think he just figured why not? Nothing to lose for him, and after all, they did snuff out one of his people last night."

"What if what he told us was bullshit, and he makes a complaint to the U.S. attorney; says we coerced him?"

The waitress poured coffee.

"As the U.S. attorney would say, that's an 'unsubstantiated allegation,'" Carr said. "Not enough evidence for prosecution. I think we would beat the rap."

$/17

It was dark. Red Diamond's insides fluttered as if a flock of birds was trying to fly out his ass.

He sat behind the wheel of the Cadillac and waited. The coffee-shop parking lot was half full. He watched the back door. It was shift-change time.

He had no particular strategy. It would be strictly "play it by ear."

Mona, looking tired, in a spotted waitress uniform, came out the back door carrying a purse. She headed for a battered Volkswagen.

Red got out of the Cadillac and rushed across the lot. He opened the car door and slid into the passenger seat.

Mona was starting the car engine. "What do *you* want?" Her jaw was set.

"I just wanted to talk for a few minutes."

"Get out of my car."

"I know what you probably think of me, but that's what I want to talk about. This last stretch has brought me to my senses. No lie. I've finally wised up." He wished she would at least look at him.

"Get out of my car." She folded her hands across her chest.

"Maybe you don't have any feeling for me now, but there was a time you did. You shouldn't forget that. You owe yourself a few minutes just to listen. For the sake of the way we used to be."

"You are a liar. You aren't capable of telling the truth. You're sick. Get out of my car."

"All I want to say is that I have some great things in the fire now, some really *positive* things. For once, I actually have cleaned up my act. I know this idea will sound far-out, but I would like to see us together again. I promise you'll be able to live well, even better than when I had the place in Long Beach. I don't like to see you slinging hash. It hurts me. You deserve better. We could move into a nice place in Burbank or somewhere right now. I've got some cash. I mean you wouldn't even have to sleep with me at this point. That would be up to you. Completely your choice."

Her face turned red. She faced him.

He stared at her panty-hosed legs, the tiny waist that his hands once fit perfectly around, the firm breasts that had been his to tease.

"Why should it make any difference if we sleep together?" she said with a strained smile.

"Well, I . . ."

"I mean, it shouldn't make any goddamn difference *who* I sleep with ever again, should it?"

"That was something . . . a one-in-a-million situation. It would *never* happen again, as God is my witness, and I wouldn't say that if I didn't really mean it. . . ."

152

"You asshole!" Tears glistened in her eyes. "You've *never* meant anything you said! You are sick! You did the one thing to me I could never forgive, and here you are back again. Maybe you've forgotten. I was your wife and you made me turn tricks to pay off *your* debts. I became a whore to save *your* ass! Not that my life had been a bed of roses . . . but I had never been a goddamn whore. Sucking off ten stinking-fat businessmen a night until I got you off the hook. *And what did you do?* Pulled another of your capers, one of your 'operations,' and you went to prison *anyway*." The tears almost jumped from her eyes.

Red put his hand on her waist. He had to touch it. It felt the same as ever. The tears were, psychologically speaking, a good sign, he thought. The barrier was breaking down.

She sobbed loudly. Suddenly, she stuck a hand into her purse and pulled out something with a red wooden handle. "Get out!" she screamed, and stabbed toward his chest with an icepick. He used his hands to shield himself. The icepick pierced his palm. "You asshole! I hate you!" Mona shrieked.

Red sprang out of the car. The ice pick was stuck through his hand. He stared at the speared hand and gave a deep animal moan. "Bitch, bitch, dirty bitch!"

Mona started the rattly engine of the VW. He jumped out of the way. The car sped out of the parking lot.

It took a few minutes to get up the courage to pull the ice pick out of the wound so he could drive himself to a hospital.

"How did it happen?" said a nurse in her thirties with a hairdo like Mona's. She pushed his hand into a mixture of hot water and disinfectant. It stung so much he almost passed out.

"Chopping ice in a freezer at a party," Red said. "Hated to leave. All my friends were there. Henry Winkler, Larry Hagman, the Gabors."

"Really?" She pulled his hand out of the water.

"Actually, they're my clients. I run an advertising agency. TV commercials, that sort of thing."

"Must be an interesting job." She smiled and filled a hypodermic syringe.

"I guess you could say that," he said.

The clerk was prematurely bald and attempted to hide the fact by wrapping his few remaining hairs in a circle on top of his head. He spoke, balancing a pipe between his teeth.

"Sorry, Charlie, I can't allow you to review any files unless you have a warrant or a subpoena. Federal Parole Office regulations in accordance with the privacy act. You know how it is." Having said this, he returned to his newspaper-covered desk and sat down.

Carr and Kelly walked past the clerk and found a file cabinet marked "D." Kelly pulled open the drawer. The clerk turned a page of the newspaper.

There were three files bearing the name Diamond. Only one was current.

Carr glanced quickly over reports in the file: "sociopathic personality," "reacts in a hostile manner," "blunted emotional effect," "lacks positive value judgement," "poor communicative skills."

He opened a large envelope stapled to the inside of the file. He removed a thick stack of typed pages titled "Counseling Session Transcript. Prisoner Rudolph Diamond (#40398654). True Name: Rudolph Spriggs." The first page was a statement signed by Diamond giving permission to record the session for "study purposes."

Carr read:

Counselor: Had this ever happened before?

Diamond: It happened a lot when I was a kid. I think it had something to do with the sound of a train whistle. This may sound weird, but my mother's house was near the railroad tracks and when a train whistle would blow I could feel it all the way through my body, sort of as if the sound entered through the hole in my pecker. I had this terrible feeling of fear at my mother's house. And the train whistle was part of it somehow. I had trouble urinating when I was afraid. That was my first memory of having problems taking a leak.

Counselor: And you believe this affected your working life?

Diamond: After I quit high school I went to work in a bottle factory in Oakland and when I went into the bathroom to piss . . . uh, urinate, I just couldn't. I couldn't relax enough to urinate when other people were around. So I quit.

Counselor: And this affected your subsequent employment?

Diamond: What would you do if you worked in a factory with one of those giant cement bathrooms? You know, lots of urinals, and every time you went in to take a leak there were other people there and you couldn't go. Like there was *no way*. Well, you'd do what I did. You'd quit. This happened to me over and over again. I couldn't hold a job and I started to get into trouble to get money. The first thing was the phony raffle tickets. I sold them and kept the money. I got caught. You can see that on my rap sheet there. I did twenty days. I was just a kid.

Counselor: Uh-huh. What were these other arrests . . . there? In the fifties.

Diamond: Pyramid schemes. You know, chain letters. At the time everyone was doing it. I didn't even know it was illegal until it was too late.

Carr skipped fifteen or so pages.

Diamond: So after I got out . . . it was my second prison sentence . . . I bought this bar in Long Beach. Nice place, but eventually guys I knew from the joint kept coming around and got me involved in phony race-track tickets. I didn't have anything to do with printing, you understand. It was a wrong-place/right-time sort of thing. They got me on a conspiracy.

Counselor: The rap sheet says accessory to murder.

Diamond: That's the way it wound up. It was an argument over the tickets. They used a gun I had behind the bar for protection. . . . I'm not trying to make excuses. I don't want you to get the wrong idea. . . .

Carr began flipping pages rapidly.

"He sounds like a confidence man," Kelly said.

"The urinary-problem act shows great imagination," Carr said. "I wonder if he got the private cell he wanted?"

Finally he found a prison status sheet signed by a counselor recommending that Diamond be provided with a single cell for medical reasons. "Here it is," he said.

Kelly laughed.

Carr flipped through to the last page of the folder. It read:

Parolee Diamond acted as a principal in a major stock swindle involving the fraudulent sale of undeveloped tracts of land near the Colorado River. During the course of this conspiracy he was also involved in a confidence scheme involving the proposed sale of nonexistent smuggled gold to a wealthy Los Angeles jeweler. Diamond and two accomplices drove the jeweler from Las Vegas to a pay phone in San Diego to await a phone call from a supposed Mexican gold smuggler, who was to deliver the contraband. The jeweler refused to part with the money in his briefcase until he saw the gold. When the phone rang, the jeweler stepped out of the vehicle to answer it. At this point Diamond and his accomplices grabbed his briefcase from him and departed in their vehicle at a high rate of speed. The jeweler fired at Diamond's vehicle with a .38 caliber revolver, wounding the driver. The driver was subsequently admitted to a hospital near San Ysidro suffering multiple gunshot wounds. He implicated Diamond and agreed to testify for the government, as did the jeweler. Federal prosecution was authorized since Diamond and his accomplices had crossed state lines during commission of the crime. Parolee Diamond was convicted on all counts and completed the full five years of his sentence, no time off for good behavior.

Carr tore Diamond's photograph from inside the folder.

"This is our man. He's a rip-off artist," Carr said. He took the mug photos of red-haired men out of his coat pocket and flipped through them.

"What are you doing?" Kelly asked.

"Diamond's picture wasn't among the photos we were checking out. We would never have found him." Carr dropped the photos into the wastebasket.

"Here's his current address." Kelly took a pen

and small note pad from his inside coat pocket. "It's 4126 Marshall Avenue. If I remember right, this should be just above Hollywood Boulevard; toiletland, U.S.A." He wrote down the address and put the note pad back in his pocket.

Carr closed the folder and put it back in the file
drawer.

"We headed for Hollywood?" Kelly smiled and
rubbed his hands.

"Not yet," said Carr, leaning against the cabinet. He stared at Diamond's mug shot. "I think
we'd better talk to the U.S. attorney."

"But we don't have enough for a warrant on
Diamond."

"We do for Ronnie, because we can identify
him. We saw him go into the motel room. We can
get a John Doe warrant for assault on a federal
officer. It's best to have the warrant in hand when
we make the pinch. Then there'll be no question
about procedure when he goes to court."

"You mean we set up a surveillance on Diamond and wait until he meets with Ronnie, *then*
make the pinch, right?"

"Right." Carr flicked Diamond's mug photo
with his finger.

"If we start a surveillance," Kelly said, "we
might end up following him around from now till

hell freezes over and he might never meet up with Ronnie."

Carr said, "What happens if we pick up Diamond and he won't talk? You know the odds. He refuses to cop out and we have to let him go; he calls Ronnie and tips him off. Ronnie splits and we'll never find him."

Kelly rubbed his eyes. "I guess you're right. I just don't like the idea of getting the mushhead U.S. attorneys in on the case too soon. You know how they are."

Carr nodded.

"Well, I guess it's up the elevator to the Ivory Tower." Kelly sighed.

They walked past the clerk.

"Wait a second, you guys!" said the clerk. "Whataya say for the game tonight? Dodgers or Pirates?"

"Pirates all the way," Carr said.

"I hope you're right. I've got ten bucks on 'em." He folded the sports page in half.

"Good luck," Carr said.

In the elevator, Kelly pushed the button for the thirteenth floor.

"Let me do the talking," Carr said.

The elevator door opened onto a large and handsomely carpeted waiting room. Smiling photos of the president and the attorney general stared at one another from spotless walls. Air conditioning made the room chilly.

A frail secretary showed them into a comfortably furnished office with a Stanford diploma on the wall. John Blair was on the phone, thick lips touching the mouthpiece. Blair was a young man with an abundance of what some would describe as baby fat: rosy cheeks, puffy neck, fraternity-house beer belly. He wore the latest gold-wire-frame spectacles. His hair was a styling-salon natural.

"Gotta go now, hon. See you at five-thirty or so, depending on the freeway, ya know." He put down the receiver and pointed to two chairs.

They sat down.

"Well, well, Charlie and Jack, the old guard of the Treasury Department." His voice was youthful. "What can I do for you this fine day?"

"I want a John Doe warrant for the guy who killed Rico de Fiore."

"Have you found the killer?" he said. He doodled on a yellow pad.

"We're starting a surveillance on a residence in Hollywood where we think he might show up. I want to have a warrant in hand when we take him just so there'll be no legal technicalities popping up later. I want to make sure there are no loopholes in this case."

"I'm glad you came in, Charlie. I've been wanting to get together with you fellas on the prosecution angle ever since it happened. There *is* a problem, ya know." He stopped doodling.

"No, I *don't* know," Carr said. "We watched this Ronnie or whoever he is walk into the motel room. We heard the shotgun. We went in the room seconds later and found Rico shot dead. If that doesn't mean a certain conviction for Ronnie when we catch him, I don't know anything about the law. Rico sure as hell didn't kill himself."

Blair scratched his natural. It appeared stiff

161

with hair spray. "No, that's not the problem. The problem is self-defense. It's a one-on-one situation, ya know."

"How do you mean?" Kelly said.

"If you arrest this Ronnie and he goes to trial, you know he can take the stand and say he drew his gun and fired in self-defense after the other man started to pull *his* gun. Rico was working undercover. He *was* acting the part of a criminal, you know? Don't forget that. All Ronnie will have to do is take the stand and admit that he is a seller of counterfeit money. He'll say that in the motel room this surly-looking Italian, whom he firmly believed to be a Mafia lieutenant, tried to steal his counterfeit money and he had to defend himself. Ya know? He might even say that Rico identified himself as a T-man and reached for his ankle gun but he didn't believe it and defended *himself* from a possible rip-off. The physical evidence shows that Rico's pants leg was up and thus he *may* have reached for his ankle gun. As you know, the defense is entitled to a copy of all the coroner's reports and everything; that's the law. They'll use whatever defense fits the facts the best. Ya know?"

Carr and Kelly sat without speaking.

Blair picked up an expensive-looking fountain pen and made ink dots on the yellow pad. When he spoke again his voice was softer.

"We have to keep in mind that there isn't even a murder weapon. Although the coroner could testify that Rico was killed with shotgun pellets, we can't actually tie Ronnie to a murder weapon. Ya know? All you saw him carry into the room was an attaché case, and he obviously took the weapon with him when he escaped. The final problem with the case is that it will be your word against his. You will be open to a tough cross-examination as to how you recognized him as the person who walked into the room, excluding all other persons who may look like him; et cetera, et cetera, et cetera. Ya know? This guy may even have a brother to bring into court that looks like him. Do you see what I'm getting at? The case is weak. I don't think we can get a conviction on murder *or* assault on a federal officer, and there is no other physical evidence of other crimes except the sample counterfeit bill he gave Rico. And that is inadmissible as evidence because Rico is . . . uh . . . not here to testify about it. Ya know?" He looked at his watch.

"If we find the shotgun, what kind of a case will we have?" Carr said, looking at Kelly.

"Not too good," Blair said flatly. "There is no way we can tie the shotgun to the crime. It's not like a pistol; ballistics doesn't do us any good with shotguns. Even if you find the shotgun, there's no way to prove it was the shotgun that killed Rico. Shotgun pellets are shotgun pellets. Ya know? It's too bad it wasn't a pistol. The case, as it stands, is almost nonprosecutable. This is a fact you will have to accept. . . . I know how you guys feel, but that's it. Ya know?"

"We'll try to dig up some more evidence through our surveillance." Carr stood up. So did Kelly.

Blair rolled his fountain pen between his hands, making a clicking sound each time it hit his oversize college ring. "Ya know it's not that I wouldn't like to give you a warrant, but there's no use arresting somebody we can't take to trial and convict. Ya know?"

They walked out of the room.

"I'm glad you held back," Carr said to Kelly.

"I'm not," Kelly said. "When I was in the police department years ago, we had a deputy district attorney like him. He refused to give my partner a complaint on a guy that slapped him in the face. The D.A. said it 'wasn't aggravated enough'; therefore it wasn't really a crime under the penal code. You know what my partner did? He slapped the D.A. in the face and knocked him clean out of his chair. You should have seen the uproar." Kelly laughed so loud the secretary put a finger in her ear so she could hear the phone.

The elevator door opened.

"What happened to your partner?" Carr said.

"Six months without pay and lost a stripe. But he always said it was worth it to him."

"A couple of years from now Blair will go into private practice and be thinking up phony defenses for his clients just like the ones he was telling us about."

"How did he ever get into the U.S. attorney's office?" Kelly said.

"Ever heard of Blair's Restaurants and Pastry Shops? Daddy Blair was invited to the inauguration."

"Oh!"

The elevator door opened.

On the way to Hollywood, Kelly insisted they stop on Alvarado at Calhoun's Hot Dog stand. Carr placed the order while Kelly pulled napkins from a dispenser and stuffed them in his pockets.

A short, fat black man wearing a sweat-stained

chef's hat wrapped everything to go. He set canned Cokes with the food in a small cardboard box and shoved it across the counter to Carr.

"Stakeout. Right?" said Calhoun.

"You guessed it," Carr said. He tried to hand Calhoun money.

The chef's rough-looking hands made a practiced "on the house" gesture. "That old Howard Dumbrowski . . . I bet he was a good man for stakeouts," he said.

"He sure was." Carr nodded.

Calhoun leaned on the counter with both arms. "Once, Howard Dumbrowski and me was sitting at that table behind you chewing the fat. It was late at night. Howard was on his way home and stopped for a coupla dogs. Hot damn if a lady don't get off a bus across the street and some six-foot-three mutha fucka snatches her purse and knocks her down. You could see she was hurt. Old Howard come off from the table like O. J. Simpson. He was across the street and had the mutha fucka by the collar before he got fifty feet. You could see the old lady had a busted arm—the bone was sticking out. I called an ambulance quick's I could." He smiled, showing a gold front tooth. "Course by the time it got here, I had to call another one for the purse snatcher. Howard was making these little screams with every punch. Had tears in his eyes. Like he was getting his nut or something. Beat that dirty mutha fucka up and down that sidewalk. All types of inspectors and shit came around the next few days. I told 'em that mutha fucka attacked Howard first and Howard just defended hisself." He lowered his voice. "The way I seen it, the purse snatcher attacked

165

Howard's fists with his head and stomach." The black man slapped a hand down on the counter and gave a high-pitched laugh that could be heard for half a block.

$/19

Using one hand to shield his binoculars from the sunlight, Carr watched Kelly as he crept past the front door of Red Diamond's apartment. It was on the second level of an unkempt avocado-colored apartment complex that was a copy of ten others on the block.

Somehow every apartment house in Los Angeles looked the same: stucco, carports, and Dempsey Dumpsters.

Kelly got back in the driver's seat. "He's living there. His name is on the mailbox. I think he's home. I think I heard a radio on inside." He opened a pop can and used the liquid to wash down a hot dog, which he devoured in four bites. He licked his fingers one by one and leaned back in the seat.

Carr continued to use the binoculars.

"He should have given the guy a dollar and told him to go find a better piece of ass," Kelly announced.

"Who?"

"Howard. That's what he should have done when he walked in on his old lady. He should have just

167

taken a dollar out of his wallet, given it to Joe the Grinder, and walked out, instead of blowing her away like he did."

"You're right," Carr said. "But that's just the way Howard is. He couldn't help himself any more than Freddie Roth could hold back if he's near a printing press and somebody offers him ten points on the dollar. Same with Rico's murderer. He'll keep going until he's stopped. . . ."

"Imagine us sitting here talking about old Howard as if he's a criminal?" Kelly said. "If he could hear us, he'd knock our heads together like two coconuts."

"He probably would," Carr said. He laughed.

Kelly closed his eyes for a few minutes. "Listen," he said without looking at Carr. "I know I'm always the one to say the wrong thing at the right time, but there's something we should work out."

"Shoot," Carr said.

Kelly wiped his hand on his shirttail and tucked the shirt back in. "I see the whole thing like this. From what the mushhead U.S. attorney said yesterday, it looks like once we find Ronnie, he is going to walk. If we arrest him, he goes to trial and beats the rap. He will have killed Rico for free. Blair is a hundred-percent right. They jury is going to be made up of a bunch of housewives who watch TV soap operas. When the judge instructs them on reasonable doubt, they are going to say, 'Gee whiz, there must be reasonable doubt because I can't imagine anyone being mean enough to blow somebody's head off.' I can see it now."

"You may be right," Carr said.

Nothing was said for a while.

"You and I have been through a lot," Kelly said finally. He was looking straight ahead. "You can trust me if you think we should go all the way on this one."

Carr put the binoculars down. "Ideas?" he said.

"If we find him—I mean, if it's just you and I alone, with no one else around—I say it's our ball game right then and there. He resists and we cancel his ticket," Kelly said. "We both shoot."

Carr put the binoculars to his eyes. He waited before speaking. "We have to be patient, Jack," he said. "We have to wait till everything is right." He put the binoculars on the dashboard. "And it's probably best if we don't talk too much about it. Eventually we may end up sitting on the lie box. It's better not to have discussed such things. You know what I mean."

"Yeah, sure," Kelly said.

When darkness fell, they parked closer to the apartment house, because of the lighting. Using the binoculars, Carr made out a soft flicker of light coming from the opening in a curtain.

"He's watching TV," he said.

"I wish he'd make a move. My ass is sore." Kelly popped open a soda. "Wouldn't it be great if the asshole would get in his car and go to a movie. We could just sit there and watch the movie, or better yet, a restaurant. . . ."

"Dream on," Carr said.

Clad only in boxer shorts, Red Diamond had been lounging on the fat, smelly sofa all day. His tiny apartment was filled with light and sound from a rabbit-eared portable television. Resting on

169

a dinette table, it provided flickering illumination for the dark, bare-floored room and two plastic-covered chairs, an open suitcase, and a phone with a cord long enough to reach the bathroom.

Red's bandaged hand throbbed with the waves of canned laughter emanating from the set.

He crawled off the couch and stretched. It was time for stomach therapy. In the undersized kitchen he pulled open the refrigerator and took out a bottle of real, not imitation, ginger ale. He opened the bottle at the sink. Throwing his head back, he opened his mouth wide and poured fully half of the icy ginger ale down his throat. The half bottle of bubbles tingled and stung all the way to his sour, rumbling stomach. He quickly placed the bottle back in the refrigerator and put his hands on his hips to wait for the belch. It came moments later as a strident, headdown bark.

The poison worry gas had been emitted. He was sure that if he had been able to get real ginger ale during the stretch in Terminal Island, his stomach problems could have been kept under control.

He went back to the sofa and fluffed up a pillow. It was getting dark outside, but he did not feel that the day had been wasted. Alone, with nothing but the television, he had been able to relax, to think. Having had time to treat his body with ginger-ale therapy, he had not had a loose bowel movement all day.

The television crackled with applause. A cuff-linked, effeminate game-show host held a housewife's hand and pointed to the stage set behind him. "You keep five hundred dollars or try for the wild-card prize in one of the boxes!" he quacked. "Take your choice of Prize *One*, Prize *Two*, or

Prize *Three!*" Chewing her fingernails excitedly, the housewife jumped up and down. Her breasts were bouncy, youthful, her waist firm. Perhaps as firm as Mona's? For the fiftieth time he saw Mona in the front seat of the car, the look in her eye as she stabbed him. The hole in his hand throbbed again.

"What will it be?" said the game-show man. "The *money* or one of the *wild-card boxes? Five hundred* dollars or a chance at gifts worth as much as *ten thousand* dollars."

"I'll keep the five hundred dollars," squealed the housewife. She chomped on her knuckles. The box opened. "A new car!" screamed the announcer.

"Dumb bitch," Red said to the television. He got up and turned it off. He knocked a dirty towel off a dinette chair, sat down, and flipped a spiral notebook that was on the table.

He closed his eyes and rubbed his temples. Then he picked up a ball-point pen and wrote the following:

RECOVERY OPERATION

The need for cash flow is now imperative, but falling back to quick con game would be disastrous because of being known by the cops. Cannot trust Gabe—he is probably a snitch; much too friendly. Only one to trust at this point is Ronnie. He has proved himself under fire. Dio's deadline is up and it means that plans must be changed to meet the current needs. Dio is to me a barrier, a stone wall that is holding up all further success. He has shown himself to be what he always has been, a person lacking full understanding of people and situations.

He is nothing more than a cheap gunsel who lucked out for a few scores and saved his money, like the peasant wop mother fucker that he is. To deal with Dio is a task requiring full commitment. Yes, an all-or-nothing is now upon me. I have survived before because of my mental speed and ability to decipher the codes of life. I picture myself at this moment as a guided missile fueled by the mental speed energy I have been able to develop using the nuclear resources of concentration. Dio's weakness is that, even in the Beverly Hills days, he accepted other people as stereotypes. He could never change an opinion of someone once it was made. His supposed mastery of power is a sham. I want to stick a burning cigar right into his eye and push it into his activating, rotten shit brain. He has challenged my energy by his failure to understand my mental speed. I must maintain control of the resources at my command in order to return to the home plate of life. I have waited five years. I have been patient. I have not been remorseful. I have not been anything other than a gentleman who requests his seat at the table back. I am fifty-four years old and the little things mean more to me now. There is no question that I can handle the problem with Mona. Time is a healer. Dio, if he was a man instead of a phony rotten prick, could give me more time by just snapping his fingers—but he won't. I have never been afraid to face the music of life. It is time for a plateau decision.

It took him almost an hour to write this. After completing it he took another ginger-ale-belch treatment. Almost simultaneous with the emission of the worry gas, as if by the magic healing properties of ginger, he was aware of what he had to do. He picked the phone up off the floor and dialed. A woman answered.

"Hello."

"I wanna speak to Tony Dio. This is Red Diamond."

A click. "Hello, Red, this in Tony. What can I do for you?"

"I know tomorrow is the deadline, but something just came up and I wanted to check and see if I could get a slight extension. This is not a stall. I give you my word on that. It's just that I'm in the middle of a project that I have capital tied up in. Right now it would be so much easier if I could just have a little more time. That way I can pull off my caper without having to shortstop the whole thing right in the middle. I'm only asking for a few more weeks."

"Are you telling me you don't have what you are supposed to have by tomorrow?"

Red hesitated. He felt as though a faucet had been turned on in his intestines. "Oh, it's not that. *Not at all*. I have the full amount that I owe you. It's just that for the moment the money is tied up in something, and if I pull the money out right now to pay you, I'll just suffer a loss of possible profit and . . ."

"I don't like to talk on the phone, Red. You know that. Tomorrow is your deadline. I will be open for business in my hotel suite tomorrow. Be there at 7:00 P.M. with the money. Bring me cash. If you aren't there, you will have visitors. Like I said, business is business. Points are points."

"After all the fuckin' years I've known you . . ."

"The story has been told, Red. School is out."

Red's stomach roared. "Okay, okay, if that's the way it's got to be . . . I'll send a guy over with the money tomorrow."

"I don't like strangers. Make sure you are with him. I don't open my door for any fucking strangers."

"All right then. I'll bring the money over, but he'll be with me. I don't like to walk around alone with that much money."

"I understand," Dio said. "See you tomorrow."

Red put the receiver down. His hand throbbed painfully. His stomach was an active, squirming bagpipe filled with worry gas and various poison body liquids. He returned to the sofa and watched television until two in the morning. When he finally got into bed, he couldn't sleep, because his mental speed would not slow down to that of an ordinary man.

By the time the sun started to come up, every muscle in Carr's body was sore.

Kelly snored himself awake in a back seat littered with empty pop cans and chili-stained napkins. He sat up and rubbed his hands roughly over his face and hair.

"Breakfast time," he said. "I'll walk down to that little restaurant at the corner." He got out of the sedan.

Less than a minute later Red Diamond walked out of his apartment and got into a Chevy parked at the curb. He started the engine, made a U turn, and headed toward Hollywood Boulevard.

Carr made the same U turn and followed a half-block behind. He slowed near the restaurant to let Kelly jump in.

"You might know he'd leave as soon as I tried to grab a bite," Kelly said.

Carr drove at a safe distance behind Diamond down a deserted Hollywood Boulevard to La Brea.

Diamond turned south and continued past motels and coffee shops, and pulled into a small shopping center.

Carr stopped farther up the street. Kelly used the binoculars.

Diamond opened the trunk of his vehicle and carrried something into the small shopping center.

"A Laundromat," Kelly said. "He's going to do his laundry. Just our luck. I know what you are going to say: 'Have patience.'"

"Time sure flies when you are having fun," Carr said. He rubbed the small of his back.

Red Diamond had a headache from lack of sleep. He shoved the bundle of clothes into the washing machine and dropped the quarters into the slot. The machine hummed.

He closed his eyes and leaned on the machine with both hands for a long while. Then he stood up straight, walked to the pay phone in the corner, dropped in a dime, and dialed.

He hung up the receiver in a moment. His head throbbed. Another dime. He dialed a number. It rang five times.

"Hello," Ronnie Boyce said. He was out of breath.

"This is Red. What are you doing?"

"Fucking and sucking about a hundred miles an hour."

175

"I gotta talk with you in person. Meet me at the Paradise Isle."

"Right on," Ronnie said. "Just as soon as I get off once more." He laughed.

Red hung up.

"He's been in there almost an hour now," Kelly said. "Maybe there's a back door. He might have gone out the back."

"Here he comes," Carr said.

Kelly started the engine.

Diamond got in his car, backed out of the parking space in front of the Laundromat, and drove south on La Brea. Kelly pulled into the flow of traffic a few cars behind him. Red turned right on Sunset Boulevard. The agents followed, making a right turn on a residential street.

"He must be heading back up to Hollywood Boulevard," Carr said. Diamond was a block ahead of them.

Suddenly an old Chrysler flew backward out of a driveway directly in front of them. Kelly slammed the G-car in reverse, backed up, and tried to get around it, but was blocked by a car parked at the curb. The blue-haired matron in the Chrysler had stalled. The street was blocked

Carr wanted to jump out and chase Diamond's car as he watched it round the corner ahead of them. It was out of sight. Kelly sped in reverse for half a block until he could turn a corner. It was too late. They had lost him.

They drove back to Diamond's apartment to see if he was there. No luck.

"We've lost him," Carr said, gritting his teeth.

"Goddamnit to hell!" Kelly exploded. "We just

176

wasted a whole day in this stinking car because of that old maid! *Sheeyit!*" He slammed a fist into an open hand.

"Let's take a shower break," said Carr. "Why don't you drop me off at my place and pick me up in a couple of hours and we'll set up again on his apartment. He's got to come back sometime."

$/20

Carr sat at a window table and watched Kelly finish eating. Kelly, with his mouth full, waved at
Prince Nikola of Serbia.

The ex-wrestler, wearing a white butcher's
apron, put a second basket of French rolls in front
of Kelly. "You eat too much bread. Pretty soon
you are three hundred pounds, like Man Mountain
Dean." He filled his cheeks with air and made a
face. "He used to get winded just climbing in the
ring." He gave a mischievous smile.

Kelly's mouth was full. He said "Fuck you, too"
in three grunts.

Nick laughed uproariously and headed toward
the kitchen.

Kelly finally swallowed. He broke another roll
in half and plastered it with butter.

Carr stared out at a mixture of people walking
in various directions carrying towels, surfboards,
and umbrellas.

"Could you recognize him?" Kelly said.

Carr didn't answer.

"I mean if he walked past the window right
now. Right this minute . . . Personally, I'm not

sure. He walked up the steps and into Rico's room. I didn't even get a face-on shot of him. I'm just not sure."

Carr continued to stare out the window. "I think I would. . . . But I'm not sure."

Kelly bit into the roll and chewed. "Maybe we're not doing the right thing."

"How do you mean?"

"I mean, maybe instead of doing surveillance on Diamond, we should just go up against him. Kick his door in and have a little heart-to-heart with him about who his young pal is. Knock his dick in the dirt if he doesn't cop out."

"If he won't cop out, we're through. We'll have tipped our hand," Carr said. "I say we watch him for a while longer."

The bar was empty. Gabe, the bartender, made squeaking noises as he dried glasses with a brownish rag. A radio broadcast race results.

Red Diamond joined Ronnie Boyce in the red leather booth. He slid across in order to sit close, pulled an ashtray toward him, and lit a cigarette. He coughed once, richly.

"You're in trouble, baby." Red took a fierce puff from his Pall Mall and turned his head to jettison a stream of smoke.

"What do you mean?" Ronnie said.

"A contract."

"On who?"

"On you."

"Who would let a contract on me?"

"Friends of the young guinea you dumped last week. Somebody fingered you." Red picked a piece of tobacco from his lower lip and flicked it away. "Somebody must have been watching when you met in the motel room. Everybody has a backup man. It's probably for sure he didn't show up alone carrying ten grand. Somebody must have seen your face and put you together someway. . . . The word is that there was a lookout near the motel who saw you walk in the room." His words ran together.

"Who told you all this?" Ronnie leaned closer to the older man.

"I got a call from a friend who's connected real good with the big boys. I've known the guy for years. He called to ask me if I wanted twenty cases of bourbon off a truck job. We're shooting the shit, see, and he asks me if I know a guy named Ronnie Boyce. Not knowing what is on his mind, I tell him no. He tells me a contract is out on a Ronnie Boyce for icing a San Fernando Valley boy in a rip-off. Seems the guinea you iced was somebody's mule. He was handling paper between here and Las Vegas for the big boys."

Ronnie rubbed his chin. "What do you think I should do?"

"Only one thing to do. Beat the fuckers to the goddamn punch. If they want to fight, I say there's no better time than the present. We move first. We show'em our shit." Red made a gun gesture with his thumb and index finger.

"What if everybody's got a baby brother?"

"I've already checked it out. The guy that put out the contract is a loner. No family ties. He's just a juice man; a ten-percent-a-week Shylock. He had the Italian kid buying hot paper for him. That's all. No family connections. Nothing like that. He wants to make himself look good by offing you. If we put him out of the way, that would be the end of it. Nobody would take his place. No baby brothers. No revenge bullshit. The problem would be solved." Red sucked in smoke.

Gabe came over with drinks on a tray and said, "Coupla usuals." He put the drinks on the table and slithered back behind the bar.

"How are we gonna do it?" Ronnie said with a puzzled expression.

"The juice man does his business out of the California Plaza Hotel. He rents a suite two days a week and people come to him to do business. This friend of mine can get me an introduction. You will be my bagman. We go to the hotel like we were going to get a loan, and do the fucker right in his room. The sawed-off piece doesn't have any numbers. Drop it in the room, and we walk out nice as can be." Red made the washing-hands gesture.

"He'll probably have a backup, right?" Ronnie said.

"Probably. If so, you'll have to dump him, too. There's no other way."

"Right," Ronnie said. His expression was placid.

"How's it sound to you?" Red said. "I mean, do you feel confident? Do you feel good about it?" He resisted the urge to pat the young man's arm.

"What's the guy's name? The loan shark," Ronnie said.

Red's voice was lowered. "Tony Dio. Ever heard of him?"

Ronnie shook his head. "No."

"Very good . . . uh . . . I mean, why should you? He's nothin'—a piece of shit." Red gulped down half of his straight soda and spat ice back into the glass.

"Red, how do you know your friend gave you the straight scoop about this thing?"

"Because I've known him for years." Red finished off the rest of the drink and wiped his mouth on the cocktail napkin. "He's solid. I trust him just like I trust you. See what I mean?"

"I see." Ronnie turned his glass on the table.

"We've got to handle this just right. I want you to go back to your motel room and wait there. Tomorrow I'll pick you up about 6:00 P.M. We pick up your piece. We drive over to the hotel and get it over with. If we're lucky, he may even have some dough in the room. If so, it'll be that much better for us. Two birds with one stone." Red smiled as hard as he could.

Carr walked up the stairs and opened the door to his partment. Magazines on the coffee table included a three-month-old journal of criminology and a couple of Sally's *Cosmopolitans*.

He showered and shaved and put on a loose-fitting shirt and slacks. He walked into the kitchen and opened the refrigerator door. Green bologna. He pushed it into the garbage-disposal.

The doorbell rang. When he opened the door, Sally looked slightly embarrassed.

"I can't believe you are home for once," she said with a half-smile.

He lowered his head to kiss, but she walked by him and went to the sofa.

She wore athletic shorts and top and tennis shoes.

"Why aren't you at work?" he said.

"Because it's Saturday. The day when normal people don't work. They ride their bikes along the beach."

"I worked all night," Carr said. "I guess I forgot what day it was."

"That's nothing new for you. A new day is a new pinch, right?" Sally slumped down on the couch.

Carr closed the door. He walked back to the refrigerator and began rummaging.

"I came over here to talk."

"Okay." He tossed out a moldy orange.

Sally folded her arms across her chest. "I've been doing a lot of thinking lately," she said. "The whole relationship is wrong. It's not based on anything permanent. We're just using one another. It's not a mature relationship. It never has been. I think it's self-destructive. You're a very cold person and I am not. I like stage plays and art galleries and you don't. I'm thwarting my own potential." She spoke as if she had written it out ahead of time.

"I see," Carr said. He closed the refrigerator door.

"You're going out with a waitress in Chinatown," she said. "You've been seen with her. Do you want to talk about it?" Her tone was schoolmarmish.

"There's nothing to talk about."

"Do you sleep with her?"

"Yes."

She chewed her lip a moment, watching him. Then she changed the subject. "You've always had the ability to judge right and wrong by your own strange set of standards. When we first met, I was

184

fascinated by that mysterious trait. Perhaps infatuated is the word I mean." She stood up and walked to the window. She stared at the beach. "Lately I feel out of place with you," she said. "As if I might have been sent from an escort service. The barrier you built around yourself gets stronger and stronger. . . ." She turned and faced him. "It's not as if we are married. I'm not some stupid, naggy housewife. I'm not chattel." Her voice cracked. "Why couldn't you have told me about her?"

Carr walked closer to her. He spoke quietly. "I didn't tell you because I didn't want to hurt your feelings."

"The same thing happened to your friend Howard. He built a barrier around himself and stopped understanding people's weaknesses. His view became distorted." She looked at her palms. "What I'm talking about is honesty between two people." She looked up. "Being able to have a meaningful dialogue."

"That's a lot of shit," Carr said without emotion.

Sally's jaw dropped.

"Those ideas come from the classes you're taking," he said. "Your teachers are phonies and faith healers whose heads are packed full of mush. They peddle bullshit to people like you, who buy it so you can have something to talk about during coffee breaks. How's that for honesty?"

"What is wrong with the truth?" Sally said.

"The truth? You tell me. You work in a courtroom all day. That's supposed to be Truth City. The only truth in there is that the judge is appointed for life."

185

"What happens in there has nothing to do with what happens between people," Sally said.

"That's my point."

"This is a stupid conversation. It's my fault. I'm playing a stupid female role." Her eyes were wet. "I came over to see if you wanted to go bike riding. I thought we could stop by Nick's for a drink on the way back." She began to cry.

Carr had a feeling of *déjà vu*—Sally with him somewhere in sleepy darkness and he was whispering things that he would never have said in the light.

A knock on the door. Carr turned from Sally and, without hurrying, walked to the door and opened it. It was Kelly.

Sally's hands flew to her face, and Kelly retreated down the stairs.

The phone rang. Sally slumped on the edge of the sofa. The sobs came in waves.

Carr picked up the receiver. "Hello."

"Delgado here. I think you're on the right track. Records at Terminal Island show that Red Diamond shared a cell for over three years with a young guy named Ronnie. Ronnie Boyce. He fits the description. We pulled his records package, and he's a bank robber. He likes the heavy stuff—a real psycho. He shanked an inmate during his second year in T. I. but they couldn't prove it. His whereabouts are unknown now. He listed a phony address when he was released."

Carr wrote the name down on a pad. "Sounds like he's our man."

"There's something else," Delgado said. "A teletype just came in. You've been transferred to Washington, D.C. You're supposed to report there

186

as soon as possible. I've stalled it by answering back that you have lease problems with your apartment. You're going to have to move fairly quickly. Sorry I couldn't tell you in person."

"Thanks, Alex." Carr put down the receiver. Sally was gone. He looked out the window. She was peddling away along the bike path.

$/21

The bank, like most of the others in Beverly Hills, was spacious and modern, with lots of glass and tapestries on the walls.

Carol, in a conservative gray wig and matching pink shirt and jacket, sat down at a desk marked NEW ACCOUNTS—IUMI ISHIKAWA. A young Oriental woman in a ponytail and sundress smiled. On the desk was a framed photo of a middle-aged Oriental couple.

"I'd like to open an account." Carol enunciated each word carefully. Rich-lady talk.

The clerk handed her a signature card. "Please fill this out."

Carol filled in the name and address and got goose bumps. She always did. It would be just her luck that someday she would forget the name on the phony driver's license. Every account meant memorizing a new name. Since 10:00 A.M., when the banks opened, she had memorized four different names and addresses, one for each bank. She had four thousand dollars in cash in her purse.

She handed the signature card back to the young woman.

"How much would you like to deposit?" She rolled the card into a typewriter.

Carol reached into her purse. "I'd like to deposit this check. It's for three thousand dollars."

Iumi Ishikawa put on her glasses and examined the check. "May I see your driver's license?"

"Certainly. Here you are."

"Thank you." She copied the driver's license number onto the signature card and laid the check in front of Carol. "Would you please second-endorse the check."

Carol held her breath, signed "Gladys T. Zimmerman," and exhaled. The goose bumps started to disappear.

"You're cold," Iumi Ishikawa said. "I think the air conditioning is on too high." She rolled a rubber stamp over the check.

"Uh . . . yes . . . uh . . . too high. I would like one thousand dollars in cash. Make the initial deposit for two thousand instead of three. I'll take the remainder in cash. I'm going to buy a used car today. Cute VW. Got it picked out already." Carol smiled pertly.

"Where did you do your banking previously?"

"In Europe. My husband is with the Foreign Service. He's teaching for a year at USC. No use buying a new car and having to sell it in a year."

The clerk wasn't listening. She was staring at the check.

"I'm sorry, Mrs. Zimmerman, but we don't usually allow cash-back transactions on an initial deposit," she said.

Carol put a hand to her chest and gave a surprised look. "Then just how are we supposed to buy the VW today? My husband will *kill* me if I don't get the money for the VW. We're buying it from a student. We're getting a very good deal. Today is Friday. The car could be *sold* over the weekend. Would you prefer that I speak with the bank manager?"

"Well, if you feel that . . ."

"That's really not necessary. Surely you can see your way to bending the rules just a litle for me. I would so appreciate it. . . . Is that a picture of your mother and father?"

"Yes, it is."

"My parents live with us. That's why we came back to the U.S., to take care of them. My mother has cancer. She has me so worried." Carol looked at the floor.

"I'm sorry," Iumi Ishikawa said.

Carol raised her head. "I assure you the check is good."

"I'll speak with the manager. I'm sure he will approve the transaction once I explain it to him." Iumi Ishikawa gave an embarrassed smile, or was it a nervous smile? She walked to the manager's desk. He was blond, tan, trim as a jogger. She talked with him briefly and came back to the desk. The manager picked up his phone and dialed.

"Is there a problem?" Carol asked, lowering her voice halfway through the sentence.

The manager stared at her while speaking on the phone. The Japanese girl stood at the desk with the check in her hands. She did not sit down.

Carol's knees were shaking.

"If you'll just wait a few minutes, the check will be approved," Iumi Ishikawa said.

"No way!" Carol lunged, grabbed the check, and ran out the glass door.

Brakes squealed as she dodged across the street. Looking behind her, Carol flung herself into a department store's revolving door. She heard a siren.

Out of breath, she mixed in with women in furs and rings, moving from table to table, picking things up and putting them down, as if browsing.

Standing behind a window display, she held up a blouse and looked across the street at the bank. The bank manager and the Japanese girl were standing outside the bank looking around.

A police car pulled up. A black policeman got out and slipped his baton into a ring on his belt. The bank manager pointed down the street toward another store. He was pointing the wrong way!

The policeman and the bank manager trotted down the sidewalk.

Carol headed toward an escalator and realized she was walking too fast. She slowed down.

In front of her was a tiered display of purses. She picked one up and studied every face near her. No one was looking. She ripped off the gray wig, stuffed it in the purse, and set it back down. She ran her hand through her hair and got on the escalator.

On the way up she had a view of the entire first floor. It had three street entrances. There was canned music and the murmur of soap-opera talk from a row of color televisions. A man and woman on TV kissed. She was safe.

If no one had seen her run into the store, they would look around for an hour or so and then go away. She breathed deeply.

She realized the check was still in her hand. She

asked a salesman where the rest room was and headed for a door near a group of sofas.

In the rest room she stuffed the check in her bra. Watching the door, she took off the pink jacket and put it in a trash can. She tucked in her blouse. Her watch said it was noon. This was as good a place to wait as any.

Two giggling salesgirls came in twenty minutes later, and Carol left the rest room.

The escalator took her to each floor. She paused at every department and made up questions for the salespeople. In the fourth-floor rest room she spent a full half hour standing in front of the mirror before anyone else came in. In linens she purchased some beach towels. They filled up a shopping bag nicely.

On the third trip down the escalator, Carol began to wonder whether the salespeople were staring at her. Or was it just her imagination? But then again, why take chances?

She looked at her watch. She had been in the store two full hours.

From the display window she could see that the police car was gone from the bank. Everything seemed back to normal. The street was crowded with shoppers.

Carol tapped a young salesgirl on the shoulder. "Excuse me, is there a back way out . . . into the parking lot?"

"Sorry, these are the only customers' doors," she said, pointing to the street entrance.

"Thank you."

A bus stopped across the street and picked up passengers. That was it! She could see a bus two blocks down. Thank God!

She joined a group of women going out the door, and walked in the oppsite direction from the bank, toward a bus bench. She sat down.

Was that a police car down the street near the bus? Jesus, it was. It was just cruising. It passed the bus and then stopped for a light. It was too late to get up and run. He would see her. Once she got on the bus she would be home free.

As the police car approached, she could see that the driver was black. She felt the goose bumps. He was pulling over to the curb in front of the bus bench. She turned her head.

The policeman got out of the car and walked around the car to her. The bus passed by.

"Ma'am?"

"Yes, officer," Carol said.

"We're looking for a lady in a pink skirt. May I ask you where you've just been?"

"Just bought some towels for the beach house." She opened the bag and smiled. "See?"

"Thank you. Would you mind walking down the street with me to the bank? It will just take a minute."

"I am in a hurry. I'd really rather not. My husband is waiting for me. He's a producer at the studios." Carol looked at her watch.

"I'm afraid you'll have to come along with me. It'll just take a minute," said the policeman.

"Well, if you insist. Would you mind carrying this bag for me?"

The policeman looked at her for a moment and gave a grudging smile. "Sure."

Carol handed him the bag and kneed him in the balls at the same time. He fell backward. There was the sound of police equipment hitting the sidewalk.

Running down the street, she pulled out the check and shoved it in her mouth. "God help me! Please don't let me go back!" She turned the corner, feet flying. The sound of running came from behind her. Suddenly a black arm clamped around her neck. Her feet stopped and flew forward. Ronnie and his towel!

Her tailbone slammed against the sidewalk. She scratched violently at the arm around her neck. The policeman's sweaty cheek touched her ear. "Spit it out, Mabel," he grunted. She tried to swallow, and a funny sound came out. The vice around her neck tightened. "Okay, bitch, you asked for it. Nighty night," said the policeman. Blackness.

Carr's eyes itched from using the binoculars. Someone once told him it was caused by the light refraction of the windshield glass. Kelly's hulk filled the back seat.

"Here comes Scarlett O'Puke," Kelly said, taking a toothpick out of his mouth. A henna-haired middle-aged woman entered her apartment.

By now each resident of the avocado apartment house had been christened by Kelly. One old man was "Mr. Spitter"; the scraggly young couple on the first floor were "John and Martha Incest"; a spindly, modish bachelor who lived next door to Diamond was "Ensign Tubesteak."

"Not one of these people goes to work. Have you noticed that?" Kelly said.

"Would you hire any of them if you were an employer?"

"Fuck no," Kelly said.

"See."

"Kelly changed the subject. "I think Red is planning a caper," he said.

"What makes you say that?" Carr said.

"He's too cautious. The only place he's been in two days was a Laundromat. He's laying low. He's building up to something. Rounders never stay in their pad unless it's for a reason." Kelly used the toothpick again.

"Don't forget," Carr said, "Waxman told us Diamond was into the sharks. Maybe he hasn't made his payment and he's worried. Besides, we don't know where he went when we lost him yesterday."

"Maybe. But I say he's getting ready for a job; thinking, planning, using his noodle. Crooks always like public places."

"Maybe so." Carr exhaled. He looked in the rearview mirror.

A sedan pulled in behind them and parked. Delgado got out and came over and leaned in the passenger window.

"The duty agent just got a call from Wilshire Division. They grabbed a paper hanger in a bank. A broad. She's singing for a deal. Says her ex-con boyfriend has a sawed-off. Here's my keys. I'll fill in here with Kelly while you go talk with her."

$122

The squad room was a jumble of desks and phones. Uniformed policemen and detectives in short-sleeved white shirts used the telephones. People, mostly black, were handcuffed to benches along the walls. The voices were profane.

Carr lit a cigarette and listened to a policeman whose skin and hair were the color of his uniform. The cop's shoes and badge were soldier-shined.

"She tried to scarf the check but I choked her and dug it out of her mouth," said the policeman. He handed Carr a clear plastic envelope containing a gnawed check. "The bank manager had just got a call from a friend at another branch who was stung by the same kind of check, same M.O. The broad—her name's Carol Lomax, by the way—just had a little bad luck. Her records package says she's on parole from Corona. Got out three months ago. . . . She's talking about a dude with a sawed-off shotgun. Since it's a federal beef, I thought I'd give you guys a call."

Carr handed back the check. "Did she give you her boyfriend's name?"

"She said his name is . . ." The policeman took

a notebook out of his shirt pocket. "Boyce . . . Ronnie Boyce."

Carr's muscles tensed. "Ronnie?"

"Why? You know the asshole?"

"Yes," Carr said.

The policeman pointed to a door with a photograph of a black-robed judge on a background of girlie-magazine crotch shots. Police art. "She's in that interview room if you want to talk with her." He turned back to writing his report.

Carr wanted to run into the room. Instead, he took a couple of deep breaths. He walked slowly to the door and opened it casually.

Carol was at the table, her head resting on her arms. The room had a table, chairs, and fiberboard walls. The ashtray on the table was overflowing, though there was a wastebasket in the corner. Next to the ashtray were a few wadded-up pieces of Kleenex with red stains. She looked up at Carr.

"You a Fed?"

Carr showed his gold badge.

Carol looked at the badge, picked up a Kleenex ball, dabbed it under her upper lip, and looked at it. Her white blouse was filthy.

"What's the matter?" Carr said.

"That cop choked me out and stuck his hand in my mouth. My gums are bleeding. First of all, before I say anything I want to know what you can do for me." She dabbed again.

"I can't make you any promises."

"I know you can't promise me that I'll get off or anything. I'm on parole. They got the check. I know I'm going back." Her lower lip trembled. She stared at the ashtray. "If I could have gotten rid of the check, they wouldn't have anything on me." The Kleenex ball touched each eye, then the nose. She cleared her throat. "What I want is a letter to the parole board saying I cooperated with the Feds. I want the letter to be in my parole file."

Carr sat down and laid his hands flat on the table. "That can be arranged," he said, "depending on what you can turn."

"How about a sawed-off shotgun?" she said. "That's a federal beef, isn't it?"

"Sure is. Where is the shotgun?"

Carol rubbed the back of her neck. "In a locker at the downtown bus depot. That's where he keeps it. This guy I know. Ronnie Boyce. He just got out of Terminal Island."

"What does Ronnie use it for?" Carr said. He drummed his fingers on the table.

Carol looked at Carr's shoulder as she spoke. "I have no idea. I don't know anything about what he does with it, and I don't want to know. I just know he has it." She crushed the Kleenex.

"Have you seen it?"

"Uh, no.

"Then how do you know he has it?"

"I mean, I've seen it, but what he does with it is his own business."

Carr picked up the brimming ashtray, walked to the wastebasket, and emptied it.

"How do you know it's in the locker?" he said, before turning around.

"He's told me that's where he keeps it, and besides, I've seen the locker key in the motel room."

Carr sat down again.

"What's the number on the locker key?"

"I don't remember." Carol picked at her face. "I don't want him to know I handed him up. He's goofy."

Carr folded his hands. "If you want to do yourself any good, Carol, you'll have to tell me where he is."

"I hope you aren't going to rush over there, break down the door, and tell him I snitched him off." Carol's front teeth were bloody pink.

Carr closed his eyes and shook his head slowly.

Carol rested her ears on her fists. "The Sea Horse Motel in Santa Monica. It's on Lincoln Boulevard. Room eleven." Her eyes searched Carr. "Now that I've told you, are you still going to write the letter? Or were you just bullshitting?"

"I'll take the letter to your parole agent myself." He took out a notebook. "What's his name?" He wrote it down and put the notebook and pencil away.

"Is there any way you could get me into a federal prison so I could do my time there? They have a lot more vocational rehab stuff."

"I don't think so," he said.

"The only reason I got caught was because of my skirt. I should of changed it," Carol said. She put her head back down.

He left the police station in a hurry, headed for Santa Monica.

Carr drove past the Sea Horse Motel to get a look. Circling the block, he put the radio microphone in the glove compartment and glanced around the interior of the car to make sure there were no signs that it was a government vehicle. He drove into the motel parking lot and parked near room eleven. In the manager's office, he rang a bell at the counter. A brown cat with a missing ear jumped off the cluttered desk. Television sounds floated from a room shielded by a grimy plastic curtain.

Carr guessed the woman who made a grand entry from behind the curtain to be over three hundred pounds. With her pink curlers and skin-tight sweater and slacks, she looked like an overinflated pool toy.

She took a register card from a drawer and handed it to him along with a pen. "You want the room for a whole night or just a short while? Reason I ask is because a short while is cheaper."

"I might be here a few days."

Her curlers moved as she furrowed her brow.

"You'll have to pay the rent each day. That'll be twelve dollars for tonight."

"Here you are. I'd like to have a room near the ice machine. That's where I parked my car." Carr pointed behind him.

"All the same to me. Here's the key to room twelve. Make sure to pay each day before noon." She pulled her sweater down to reach the horizon of her pants. The sweater popped back up an inch. She disappeared behind the plastic curtain.

Carr walked into room twelve, carrying a Handie-Talkie in a brown paper sack, and sat down at the tiny dressing table with a phone on it. He removed the Handie-Talkie and turned the volume on low.

He held it close to his mouth and pressed the transmit button.

"Nine bravo four seven, this is three tango three one." He turned up the volume slightly.

"This is nine bravo four seven, go ahead."

"Two two this number"—he pulled the telephone closer—"787-9517."

"Wilco. Four seven out."

He turned off the Handie-Talkie and waited, looking at the double bed with white chenille bedspread and the circus-clown prints on each wall. A heater protruded from the wall adjoining room eleven. Above it was a vent.

The phone rang.

"Hello, Alex?"

"Where are you?"

"Sea Horse Motel on Lincoln is Santa Monica. Room twelve. Ronnie's staying in eleven. His girlfriend copped. Says he has a sawed-off. I haven't seen him yet."

"Red is still in his apartment. I'll go back to the office. Jack will stay here on Diamond. At this point, the fewer people we have involv . . ." Delgado cleared his throat. "Let me know if you need anything."

Carr hung up the phone and switched off the light. In semidarkness he moved the chair next to the wall heater. He stook on it and, being as quiet as possible, used a flat key to remove the screws from the vent. He took it off the wall and tossed it on the bed.

Through the wire vent cover on the wall of the next room he saw a mirror. In the mirror was a reflection of the man who killed Rico lying on the bed smoking a cigarette.

$123

Kelly peered through the binoculars at Red Diamond's front door. He said out loud, "Come on out and go somewhere, you dirty son of a bitch." He could hardly believe it when a moment later Diamond appeared. He started the engine.

Diamond backed his red Chevrolet out of the carport. Kelly ducked down on the seat as the car went past. Once Diamond had turned onto Hollywood Boulevard, Kelly made a tire-squealing U turn and picked up speed. He had to make the same stop-light as Diamond.

Diamond turned north on Gower, passing a group of teenagers in transparent blouses. He sloped down between green landscaping to the Hollywood Freeway.

Kelly smiled. Diamond didn't know he was being followed. Kelly stayed way back, shielded himself behind other cars.

Diamond continued to the Harbor Freeway, then veered where the high green sign said SANTA MONICA FREEWAY. Kelly grabbed the microphone from the glove compartment as Diamond swung his car off at Lincoln Boulevard.

"Three tango three one, this is your old partner. My man's coming atcha. We're a couple minutes away. . . ."

Carr's Handie-Talkie was clipped to his belt. He pressed the transmit button twice to acknowledge Kelly's message. He continued to peer through the vent. The tin edge was marking his forehead. His eyes and nose were completely inside the vent opening. He knew full well this was a violation of law. He could hear the judge now. "The defendant had a reasonable expectation of privacy as he relaxed in his room. If the agent could have observed him without removing the vent cover, he wouldn't have violated his constitutional rights. But since the agent removed the vent he infringed . . ."

"We just pulled into the motel," Kelly said.

A knock on the door. Ronnie sat up, swung his feet to the floor, crossed to the door, and opened it.

Red Diamond looked pale. "How ya feeling, baby?"

"Fine," Ronnie said. He backed up. Red came in. Ronnie shut and locked the door.

Red rubbed his hands nervously and looked around. "Where's your old lady? I been wanting to meet her."

"She went out to down some paper," Ronnie said. "Have a seat."

"Do you have any questions?" Red sat down but got right up again. "We should get going."

"Yeah. How does this guy know my name?" Ronnie pulled on pants and shirt. "You and me were the only ones who—"

Red had turned on the radio. Rock-and-roll drowned out Ronnie's words.

Carr turned his ear toward the vent, but it didn't help.

Ronnie walked into the bathroom. Red paced and bit his nails. Ronnie came out a few minutes later, shaved and combed. He sat down on the bed and put on his shoes while Red kept talking to him. He nodded his head over and over again.

Ronnie got off the bed, collected his wallet and change from the dresser, and put them in his pocket.

Red flipped off the radio.

"Where are we going?" Ronnie asked.

"He's in room twelve nineteen at the plaza penthouse. I called the hotel just a few minutes ago. I've been there before. There's a fire exit at either end of the hallway. When it's over, we can go down the steps to the next floor and get the elevator there. We'll have our car in the big parking lot outside. We can hop back on the freeway before the cops have a chance to get there."

Ronnie picked up a bottle of after shave from the dresser, poured, and slapped it to his face with both hands. "How much money do you think he'll have in the room?" He capped the bottle again.

"Probably a real load," Red said. "But no matter what, Dio must be snuffed. Him *and* his fucking gunsel. It's them or us. They may know what you look like, so get your piece out as soon as we go in the door. Get the drop on 'em, and we'll search the place. Once we find his poke, dump both of 'em right then, wipe the shotgun, drop it, and we get the fuck out." Red fumbled in his shirt pocket for a Pall Mall and hung it on a sticky lower lip.

"I still can't figure out how they knew it was me last week," Ronnie said.

"Don't matter. They did." The Pall Mall jiggled as Red talked. He looked at his watch, lit the cigarette, and coughed a few times. "We gotta get going."

Ronnie shrugged into a jacket, and they walked out the door.

Carr said, "Pick me up," into the Handi-Talkie.

Diamond and Boyce drove onto Lincoln Boulevard as Kelly pulled in the back entrance of the motel parking lot. Carr ran outside and jumped in.

"Don't lose 'em now, Jack."

"Any ideas where they're going?" Kelly said. He stepped on the gas.

"My guess is the downtown bus depot to pick up the sawed-off."

"Jesus!" Kelly kept his eyes on the road. "Could you hear them talking in there? What'd they say?"

Carr didn't answer.

The traffic was stop and go all the way downtown. Diamond pulled up in front of the bus depot and parked. Boyce got out and went in the main entrance. He blended in with a crowd of old people, sailors, and Mexican illegals.

Carr followed him through the waiting area, then lost sight of him when a group of children rushed by. He was gone.

Carr grabbed a bus driver by the arm and asked where the rental lockers were. He rushed up to the banks of lockers and almost bumped into Boyce removing a heavy black attaché case from a locker. The young man looked around nervously.

Putting the case under his arm, he strode carefully, slowly back toward the main entrance.

Carr rushed out of the depot and got back in the front seat with Kelly.

"He picked up his piece," Carr said.

Kelly's eyes were big. He reached for the microphone.

Carr grabbed his hand. "No," he said.

"But shouldn't we tell . . . ?"

Carr shook his head. He stared at Diamond's vehicle, parked up the block. Boyce sauntered out of the depot, the case still under his arm, and got in Diamond's car.

Kelly spoke harshly. "I say let's take him right *now*. He's in possession."

Carr kept his eyes on the other vehicle. Diamond started up and pulled slowly around the corner. Kelly followed.

"I think we should wait," Carr said. "Nothing to lose by waiting a little while."

"Fuck waiting," Kelly said. "Let's turn 'em off the road. Right now. If he so much as looks at his attaché case, I'll waste both of them."

"It's not time yet." Carr had his eyes on Diamond's Chevy. Back onto the freeway. Kelly's Irish face was red now, as red as Carr had ever seen it. Kelly kept glancing at Carr as he changed lanes to keep up with Diamond. The red Chevy cruised smoothly in and out of traffic and got off at National Boulevard.

"What the hell is wrong with you?" Kelly said. "I hope you're ready to take the responsibility if this freak stops right now, sticks up a liquor store, and kills the owner. You're acting strange. What's wrong? Maybe you've lost your nerve, but I

207

haven't. We've fooled with these animals long enough. I want to stop 'em and finish the thing here and now."

Carr continued to look at the road.

Diamond's Chevy took a right turn into a hotel parking lot. Carr picked up the binoculars. Boyce did something with the case on the front seat of the car. He threw some crumpled pink paper out of the passenger window.

"You follow them in," Carr said. "I'll meet you in the lobby." He flung open the car door and, being careful to stay out of sight of Boyce and Diamond, ran across the crowded parking lot and into the plush, modern hotel lobby. He found a telephone, picked up the receiver, and dialed.

Ronnie ripped off the last bit of pink wrapping paper. His hands felt sweaty. He pulled the beaver tail back, noted that a twelve-gauge round was chambered and ready to fire. He flicked off the safety. He laid the weapon back in the case and closed the lid gently, clicking only one latch.

"Got any ear plugs?"

"What?"

"Ear plugs. My ears rang for two days when I did that guy in the hotel room. This sawed-off is a loud mutha-fuckin' piece." He was making a joke.

Red forced a laugh. He slapped the young man's thigh. "Ear plugs, ear plugs." He chuckled nervously. "That'd be a real friggin' tip-off, wouldn't it? To walk in wearing a set of ear plugs." His stomach made a powerful growl. He rubbed his navel.

Ronnie stared blankly at the hotel. "I once

208

robbed a bank on the same day I was released from Chino. I took the bus from the pen and got off in San Gabriel. I picked up a piece a guy was holding for me, and stuck up the first bank I saw, then caught another bus. My parole was revoked two months later for some minor shit, but they never made me on that bank job. Never. It was as if it was free. You know, like you do five and get one free. I had a real good feeling for that job, just like I do today. I just knew things were right."

"It's confidence, baby. It's because you've got a whole bucket of balls. That's why you and your old Red buddy are going to move up the ladder. Because of mental speed and balls. There is nothing, I mean *nothing* we can't do. We've got what it takes. The ingredients are there." Red looked at his watch. "It's ten minutes to seven. Any questions, baby?" He cleared his throat.

Ronnie shook his head no. He followed Red into the hotel lobby.

At a bank of elevators, Red pushed an Up button and put his arm around Ronnie. In a fatherly manner he whispered, "You've got to get the drop on 'em as soon as we're inside. That's the important thing. As soon as we clear the door. I know you can do it, babe."

Ronnie smiled. The elevator door opened. They stepped in. So did a bellhop with a tray, and two men in sports coats. One man looked seedy. Had they met him in Terminal Island?

Inside the elevator Red pushed the button for the twelfth floor. The elevator rose smoothly, stopping twice to let off the others.

At the twelfth floor, they got out of the elevator

and walked along the hallway to the door of room twelve nineteen. It was open an inch. Red knocked lightly.

"Red, is that you?" The voice was from another room in the suite. "Come on in! I'm just getting dressed!"

Red pushed the door open slowly. He nodded to Ronnie. Ronnie stepped in first, his feet sinking into the thickest carpet he had ever felt.

"Now!" whispered Red. "Get it out!"

Ronnie unlatched the case. The shotgun was in his hands. He crept through the living room, Red following close behind. They were at the bedroom door when Tony shouted matter-of-factly, "Come on in here, Red."

Ronnie's fists gripped the shotgun firmly. His finger caressed the trigger.

Red leaned against the doorjamb and turned the doorknob. The door flew open violently.

Explosions of steel fire crashed through Ronnie Boyce's teeth and chest. He was on the floor, sinking into the carpet. Bullets were deep in his chest and head.

More explosions. Red gave a woman's scream.

Blood surged into Ronnie Boyce's mouth and lungs. He felt nausea, then dizzyness. His tongue was keeping air from his lungs. He tried to move his head to the side but it didn't work. Ruined. More ripping explosions. There was only blackness.

Carr, with Kelly two feet behind him, burst from the stairwell door holding his revolver in combat stance. Approaching the room door, he saw a bullet hole.

"Let's kick it," Kelly said.

"Take cover! They'll be bailing out!"

They hugged the walls on either side of room twelve nineteen.

Down the hallway a woman's voice shrieked, "Operator! People are shooting guns! Send the police!"

The two men who stumbled out of the room were not Boyce and Diamond. They ran toward the elevators. Carr and Kelly cut them off. "Federal officers, lads," Kelly said. "Down on the floor and spread."

After handcuffing both men and securing them in a room a maid had been working in, Carr went back to the room where the shots had been fired. He pushed open the door carefully with his revolver. Red Diamond lay next to the sofa, face down, feet twitching. Boyce was sprawled on his back in front of the bedroom door, the shotgun next to him. Carr bent down. His hand moved to Boyce's throat to test for a pulse.

He pulled the hand back before touching, stood up, walked to the phone, and dialed. "Let me have Central Homicide."

A half hour later Detective Higgins arrived. He looked at the bodies and went into the room where Kelly and a uniformed policeman held Tony Dio and his stocky bodyguard. Carr followed.

"I'll tell you exactly what happened," Dio said to Higgins as he sat on the bed. "Two bastards come up to my room to snuff out me and my friend here and we defended ourselves. I got a right to have a gun. It's registered. I was in my own hotel room. They came to do me in. To waste me." His hands were shaking.

"What happened?" Higgins said to Dio.

Carr leaned against the wall with Kelly.

"We were sitting in my room having a drink and I get a phone call. I didn't know who it was. Man's voice. He says, 'This is a friend. Red Diamond and another guy are coming up to your room to rip you off. The guy with Red has a sawed-off in an attaché case.' Then he hangs up."

Kelly's jaw dropped. He turned toward Carr.

Higgins made notes on his clipboard. "So what did you do then?" he said.

"Me and my friend here go in the bedroom and wait. My friend's got a piece because I carry large amounts of cash now and then." He looked at the bodyguard. "L.A. is a high-crime area, right? I peek out the bedroom door and I see these two guys come in the front door. One guy is carrying a sawed-off piece. So my friend here opens the bedroom door and lets loose. I mean, what would you do? It was simple self-defense."

"That's what it sounds like," Higgins said. "I'll have to ask you to come down to the station to make a written report, but by the physical evidence, it looks like self-defense. The dead guys did have a shotgun. No charges will be filed."

Higgins stepped out into the hallway. Carr and Kelly followed.

"We had Diamond and Boyce under surveillance," Carr said. "That's how we happen to be here."

"That's all I need for my report," said the detective. He walked across the hall into the room with the bodies.

It was four hours before the case was wrapped up.

Delgado arrived and chewed Rolaids while Carr explained what had happened. Per standard operating procedure, Carr and Kelly wrote statements, which would serve as their report of investigation. The statements were concise and almost identical. "Occurrence during a Routine Surveillance" was the title block.

Delgado headed back for the field office to send a teletype to Washington, D.C.

They checked the serial numbers of the money in Ronnie Boyce's wallet and found that the numbers on his six tens and two fives matched Rico's money.

Higgins unloaded the sawed-off shotgun and put it in a plastic evidence bag.

The bodies were removed to the L.A. county morgue.

After all the details were completed, Kelly suggested Ling's. Carr accepted.

The drive to Chinatown was pleasant. Little or no traffic, and the heat wave seemed to have given way to cooling, smogless sea air.

"The wife and I are thinking of having a little get-together at my place for you before you go," Kelly said. "You know, steaks and beer. I figured I'd ask five or six couples. Ling and his wife said they'd like to come. Couple of the narcs."

"That'll be real nice," Carr said. "I'll bring Sally, if she still wants to see me."

Kelly stopped for a red light at Hill and Alpine and looked both ways. He drove through before the light changed. Down the street he pulled into a curb parking space two doors from Ling's.

"Charlie," Kelly said.

"Yes?"

"How did you know that Boyce was . . ." He turned off the engine. "Oh, never mind."

They got out of the car.